While Bugles Blow!

SELECTED FICTION WORKS BY
L. RON HUBBARD

FANTASY
The Case of the Friendly Corpse

Death's Deputy

Fear

The Ghoul

The Indigestible Triton

Slaves of Sleep & The Masters of Sleep

Typewriter in the Sky

The Ultimate Adventure

SCIENCE FICTION
Battlefield Earth

The Conquest of Space

The End Is Not Yet

Final Blackout

The Kilkenny Cats

The Kingslayer

The Mission Earth Dekalogy*

Ole Doc Methuselah

To the Stars

ADVENTURE
The Hell Job series

WESTERN
Buckskin Brigades

Empty Saddles

Guns of Mark Jardine

Hot Lead Payoff

A full list of L. Ron Hubbard's
novellas and short stories is provided at the back.

*Dekalogy—a group of ten volumes

L. RON HUBBARD

While
Bugles
Blow!

GALAXY
PRESS

Published by
Galaxy Press, LLC
7051 Hollywood Boulevard, Suite 200
Hollywood, CA 90028

Printed in the United States of America.

ISBN-10 1-59212-298-1
ISBN-13 978-1-59212-298-1

Library of Congress Control Number: 2007903543

Contents

Stories from Pulp Fiction's Golden Age

A ND it *was* a golden age.

The 1930s and 1940s were a vibrant, seminal time for a gigantic audience of eager readers, probably the largest per capita audience of readers in American history. The magazine racks were chock-full of publications with ragged trims, garish cover art, cheap brown pulp paper, low cover prices—and the most excitement you could hold in your hands.

"Pulp" magazines, named for their rough-cut, pulpwood paper, were a vehicle for more amazing tales than Scheherazade could have told in a million and one nights. Set apart from higher-class "slick" magazines, printed on fancy glossy paper with quality artwork and superior production values, the pulps were for the "rest of us," adventure story after adventure story for people who liked to *read.* Pulp fiction authors were no-holds-barred entertainers—real storytellers. They were more interested in a thrilling plot twist, a horrific villain or a white-knuckle adventure than they were in lavish prose or convoluted metaphors.

The sheer volume of tales released during this wondrous golden age remains unmatched in any other period of literary history—hundreds of thousands of published stories in over nine hundred different magazines. Some titles lasted only an issue or two; many magazines succumbed to paper shortages during World War II, while others endured for decades yet. Pulp fiction remains as a treasure trove of stories you can read, stories you can love, stories you can remember. The stories were driven by plot and character, with grand heroes, terrible villains, beautiful damsels (often in distress), diabolical plots, amazing places, breathless romances. The readers wanted to be taken beyond the mundane, to live adventures far removed from their ordinary lives—and the pulps rarely failed to deliver.

In that regard, pulp fiction stands in the tradition of all memorable literature. For as history has shown, good stories are much more than fancy prose. William Shakespeare, Charles Dickens, Jules Verne, Alexandre Dumas—many of the greatest literary figures wrote their fiction for the readers, not simply literary colleagues and academic admirers. And writers for pulp magazines were no exception. These publications reached an audience that dwarfed the circulations of today's short story magazines. Issues of the pulps were scooped up and read by over thirty million avid readers each month.

Because pulp fiction writers were often paid no more than a cent a word, they had to become prolific or starve. They also had to write aggressively. As Richard Kyle, publisher and editor of *Argosy*, the first and most long-lived of the pulps, so pointedly explained: "The pulp magazine writers, the best of them, worked for markets that did not write for critics or attempt to satisfy timid advertisers. Not having to answer to anyone other than their readers, they wrote about human beings on the edges of the unknown, in those new lands the future would explore. They wrote for what we would become, not for what we had already been."

Some of the more lasting names that graced the pulps include H. P. Lovecraft, Edgar Rice Burroughs, Robert E. Howard, Max Brand, Louis L'Amour, Elmore Leonard, Dashiell Hammett, Raymond Chandler, Erle Stanley Gardner, John D. MacDonald, Ray Bradbury, Isaac Asimov, Robert Heinlein—and, of course, L. Ron Hubbard.

In a word, he was among the most prolific and popular writers of the era. He was also the most enduring—hence this series—and certainly among the most legendary. It all began only months after he first tried his hand at fiction, with L. Ron Hubbard tales appearing in *Thrilling Adventures*, *Argosy*, *Five-Novels Monthly*, *Detective Fiction Weekly*, *Top-Notch*, *Texas Ranger*, *War Birds*, *Western Stories*, even *Romantic Range*. He could write on any subject, in any genre, from jungle explorers to deep-sea divers, from G-men and gangsters, cowboys and flying aces to mountain climbers, hard-boiled detectives and spies. But he really began to shine when he turned his talent to science fiction and fantasy of which he authored nearly fifty novels or novelettes to forever change the shape of those genres.

Following in the tradition of such famed authors as Herman Melville, Mark Twain, Jack London and Ernest Hemingway, Ron Hubbard actually lived adventures that his own characters would have admired—as an ethnologist among primitive tribes, as prospector and engineer in hostile climes, as a captain of vessels on four oceans. He even wrote a series of articles for *Argosy*, called "Hell Job," in which he lived and told of the most dangerous professions a man could put his hand to.

Finally, and just for good measure, he was also an accomplished photographer, artist, filmmaker, musician and educator. But he was first and foremost a *writer*, and that's the L. Ron Hubbard we come to know through the pages of this volume.

This library of Stories from the Golden Age presents the best of L. Ron Hubbard's fiction from the heyday of storytelling, the Golden Age of the pulp magazines. In these eighty volumes, readers are treated to a full banquet of 153 stories, a kaleidoscope of tales representing every imaginable genre: science fiction, fantasy, western, mystery, thriller, horror, even romance—action of all kinds and in all places.

Because the pulps themselves were printed on such inexpensive paper with high acid content, issues were not meant to endure. As the years go by, the original issues of every pulp from *Argosy* through *Zeppelin Stories* continue crumbling into brittle, brown dust. This library preserves the L. Ron Hubbard tales from that era, presented with a distinctive look that brings back the nostalgic flavor of those times.

L. Ron Hubbard's Stories from the Golden Age has something for every taste, every reader. These tales will return you to a time when fiction was good clean entertainment and the most fun a kid could have on a rainy afternoon or the best thing an adult could enjoy after a long day at work.

Pick up a volume, and remember what reading is supposed to be all about. Remember curling up with a *great story.*

—Kevin J. Anderson

KEVIN J. ANDERSON *is the author of more than ninety critically acclaimed works of speculative fiction, including* The Saga of Seven Suns, *the continuation of the Dune Chronicles with Brian Herbert, and his* New York Times *bestselling novelization of L. Ron Hubbard's* Ai! Pedrito!

While Bugles Blow!

CHAPTER ONE

The Lieutenant Gets a Problem

THERE is, *mon Lieutenant*," said Sergeant Germaine, saluting, "a disturbance in town." The Lieutenant glanced up from his report and looked steadily at Germaine for the space of ten seconds.

"What kind of a disturbance?"

"Schmaltz was just out and he said Berbers were pouring into the public square. I thought it would be a good idea to take a squad and a Hotchkiss—"

"You're not paid to think," said the Lieutenant. "What good would a Hotchkiss and a squad do against a few thousand Berbers?"

Germaine's bristly beard bobbed up and down as he sought for words. He had a horrible idea of what the Lieutenant was about to say and do.

"Some gunner," said the Lieutenant, "might get excited and shoot a Berber and then where would we be? You know, Sergeant, that it would take a week's fast marching over the Atlas for any part of the main command to reach us."

"*Oui, mon Lieutenant,*" said Germaine. "Too well I know that. I have nightmares about it."

"We cannot start something we cannot finish."

The Lieutenant rose from the desk, buttoned his tunic collar, picked up his riding crop and put his kepi on his head. He gave the sergeant a crooked grin. An impulsive, devil-may-care fellow, this lieutenant, thought the sergeant, but a fighter. Every inch of his six feet a fighter. *Shaitan*, said the Arabs and Berbers, had molded the Lieutenant's brain; angels had fashioned his face.

"I'll go down and see what the trouble is, Sergeant."

"No!" cried Germaine. "They might mob you and kill you and then where would we be?"

"What would you do if I did get killed?" said the Lieutenant.

"I'd . . . I'd take every mother's son in this fort and rip the heart out of every Berber in Harj. That's what I'd do."

"Oh, no, you wouldn't, Sergeant. You'd stay right here in the fort, try to get a man through to the main command and get help. Those are your orders. Sergeant, I was given sixty Legionnaires and I was told to hold Harj for France. Those orders apply to you."

Germaine shifted uneasily from one foot to the other. Big and strong, he had one allegiance only—to the Lieutenant, and to hell with France or anything else.

"The main command," said the Lieutenant, "took Harj and we garrison it. If we are killed, they take Harj again which would cost an unreasonable number of lives. No, Sergeant, if anything should happen to me, you stay here at your post and let the main command do the thinking. Lieutenants, after all, are very cheap."

He went toward the door, but the sergeant blocked his way. "You must take a revolver at least, *mon Lieutenant*."

"I might shoot somebody with it. If I appear down in

4

Harj without side arms they will think me very brave. If a squad appeared they would think that we are afraid of what might happen to us. And anyway, Sergeant, this is so much dramatics. Probably they were getting ready for prayers and Schmaltz would certainly know nothing about *that*."

The sergeant grinned. The Lieutenant went down the steps and across the compound to the gate of the ancient fort. The sentries saluted as he went through and wondered greatly at the Lieutenant's lack of side arms.

Newly conquered Harj was a bomb with a lighted fuse. No roads led to it from the north. It was isolated and dangerous. The main command, unable to spare men enough to keep communication lines open all the way across the Atlas, had thought it wise to at least make a gesture at holding the place. Lieutenants were cheap. Sixty Legionnaires were cheaper.

A suicide post.

A glory or a grave-maker.

Harj was a good-sized city, teeming with tribesmen from the hills, Arabs from the lowlands. Its face was baked by the desert, its back, like a man before an old-fashioned fireplace, was chilled by the high, looming Atlas. Fertile and rich, the possible occupation of it was well worth a lieutenant and sixty men.

The Lieutenant passed the Berbers and Arabs in the crooked streets. They saluted him and he gave some slight attention to those who looked prominent or who wore a cleaner, better turban or a more stiffly embroidered djellaba.

They seemed, when he faced them, friendly enough, but

behind his back they were hard and silent. They did not like a conqueror, these free sons of the mountains. They marveled that they allowed themselves to be held by one officer and sixty men. They failed to understand that the beating they had taken from the main column would be instantly repeated if anything happened to the garrison.

An old, bearded man, walking with a limp, dressed in rags, carrying the nose of his race carefully hidden in the hood of his dirty djellaba, came abreast of the Lieutenant.

"*Monsieur,* my name is Ibn Batuta. You . . . you must excuse my appearance, though I am really not so rich as the caid pretends, but . . . you understand, Lieutenant, that one must be very careful amid these infidels. . . . I ask but little, *mon commandant*. I am a poor man, but, that is, if you should happen to need a few thousand francs. . . ."

The Lieutenant nodded. The old man smiled and drifted slowly away and, when the Lieutenant was far enough ahead, began to follow him.

The Lieutenant paused in the public square and looked about him. Battlements made a black Grecian pattern against the steel blue sky. Minarets reared curious heads and glittering half-moons far above the town.

Men were gathering somewhere near. The Lieutenant could hear a sharp, buzzing clamor near at hand. Suddenly a voice stood out, crying in Shilha, "How much am I bid? How much for this lovely article? Ah, you will beggar me. Such a bid is not worthy of you. . . . Come, how much? . . ."

The Lieutenant stepped around the edge of a garden wall

and saw that an auction of some sort was in progress in the marketplace. The shifting patterns of color in the crowd attracted him and he moved nearer.

The outer fringe, glancing backward, hurriedly made way for him and then closed behind him. Without any actual effort of his own he was rapidly propelled toward the front. Out of respect for him, in spite of the jam, they left a circle some ten feet in diameter about him.

He stood there, looking up at the stone block, crop under his arm, square-topped, straight-billed hat rakish upon his head, breeches and medals and tunic and braid putting the best dressed about him to shame.

His face was alert and interested. A sparkle of humor was deep in his gray eyes. A Frenchman would not have done this, but he was not French. A man afraid of his post and security would scarcely have allowed himself to be so surrounded and blocked off from all possible help, and the Arabs and Berbers knew, thereby, that he was a brave man.

The auctioneer had several cages behind him, shut off from view by long drapes, and the Lieutenant was far from guessing their contents until the next article was brought out to be sold under the hammer.

It was, the Lieutenant saw with a shock, a woman.

"And this choice article," bellowed the auctioneer, stomach shaking up and down every time he uttered a word. "How much, my brothers, how much? See! She is perfect in every detail. She is one of the finest women those devil-begotten Jeppas ever bred. And, my brothers, despite their low fighting qualities, not one of us will deny that the Jeppas breed excellent women!"

The crowd thought this very funny and laughed excessively. The auctioneer was in fine form now. For a moment he had lost their interest due to the Lieutenant's coming.

"I guarantee, my brothers," roared the auctioneer, "that this woman is perfect in every detail. She is beautiful and untouched. How much am I bid?"

The Lieutenant's thoughts did not show on his face. He was thinking that France did not allow this any more and that, indeed, the practice was thought to be totally extinct. But Harj was not conversant with the laws of France and the Lieutenant was hardly in a position to inform them that this was against the law of a country they had never seen and of which they had only heard the vaguest rumors.

An offer came from the crowd.

The girl, standing there stripped before this barrage of eyes, hung her head. Her hair was long and brown and fell so as to partly hide her delicately featured face. Her eyes, blacked with kohl, flicked upward every few seconds to look at the men who bid for her.

"A rotten shame," thought the Lieutenant.

Offers were buffeted about. The auctioneer bellowed and roared, told funny stories, extolled the virtues of Jeppa women and finally brought a bidder up to a good price.

The money was paid on the spot. The big-chested, hairy-faced Berber took his merchandise. The girl, to the Lieutenant's surprise, went willingly enough.

"And now!" cried the auctioneer. "We have the best of the lot. I have here a jewel, a flame-colored flower, worth a sultan's ransom. Untouched, pure as spring water, brought up in the harem, the very harem of Kirzigh himself. She is the finest of all. When she looks at you, you think two moons have risen. When she sighs you think the gentle breezes have cooled your brows. When she talks you think that nightingales have swarmed down from the heavens. She is a gift of Allah, more beautiful than the houris themselves. Her waist could be encircled with the smallest hand. A glimpse of her face and figure would pull a dead man from his shroud. And her hair! It is the color of the dawn, of the evening. It is the color of silk beyond value. It is a crown of molten gold flowing across her milk white shoulders. My brothers, gaze upon this woman and be confounded!"

He threw back a drape, dramatically bringing forth another article.

The Lieutenant had, until now, thought that this was just some pat speech of the auctioneer's. The Lieutenant had seen many, many Arab and Berber women. Some of them were very pretty, yes, but not like this one.

My God, no!

She was all the auctioneer said and more, and the Lieutenant began to think poorly of the auctioneer's oratorical abilities.

She was beautiful, but the mention of it made that word pale and insipid.

In all his life, in magazines, on the screen, the Lieutenant had never beheld such a face or such a figure.

9

Her hair was golden red, her eyes were clear and alive and gray. She looked down into the crowd as though she gazed upon so many mangy camels.

The crowd said not a word. Not one man there breathed for the space of a dozen heartbeats.

Suddenly an engulfing roar soared skyward. They slapped each other and slapped themselves and laughed and cheered and howled with pleasure.

The auctioneer, conscious that he had done something great, puffed up considerably, stroked his beard and waited for them to grow quiet.

The girl was haughty and unafraid. It was her voice which struck the crowd into silence.

"What one among you dares make a bid for Morgiana, Buddir al Buddor, daughter of the Caid?"

They gaped at her. Never in the history of Harj had a woman captive had the courage to speak from the auction block.

"Why don't you bid?" she cried. "Look at me. I am beautiful. I am worth ten thousand pieces of gold. Buy me as you buy a camel or a barb. Bid, beasts, and show me which one among you wants me the most."

For seconds nothing sounded but the clattering of palms in the public square. Then a stately Berber stepped forward and cried, "One hundred pieces of gold I bid for the honor of breaking that woman's spirit."

Another voice roared, "Two hundred pieces of gold."

A third cried, "Three hundred."

10

The first bidder, stroking his beard, looked up at the girl thoughtfully.

She called to him. "Am I not worth it? Will you not bid five hundred, you malformed ox? Bid and show them, and then I'll show you which one of us is broken first."

The Lieutenant was still dazed. His heart was beating queerly and gave little bumps every time her white teeth flashed. Then he tried to catch hold of himself. This was no way for the conqueror of Harj to act. No way at all.

He felt something press against his side. His fingers closed on a terrific weight. He glanced down.

Just as though some spirit had come to him unseen and had departed without noise, he found himself possessed of a big sack. It jingled.

"Bid!" cried the girl. "Buy me for a bargain at ten thousand pieces of gold. Ah, you're afraid. Afraid I might tear your eyes out of your heads and pluck your beards, hair by hair. We'll see about that. Bid!"

The Lieutenant raised the bag to shoulder height. The auctioneer stared blankly at him and at the sack.

The Lieutenant threw the money to the block. The bag broke and gold scattered over it like a torrent of sunlight.

The auctioneer's helpers dashed forward and scooped up the wealth. To their practiced eyes, it amounted to some seven or eight hundred pieces of gold.

The crowd cheered. In the middle of a nightmare, the Lieutenant stepped up, took the girl's hand in his own and tried to pull her away with him.

The Lieutenant threw the money to the block. The bag broke and gold scattered over it like a torrent of sunlight.

She stood where she was. He touched her again and their eyes met and clashed.

Suddenly she seized his hand, jerked it toward her and sank her teeth in it to the bone.

The sudden pain of it made the Lieutenant strike. The girl reeled back, dropping his hand. He looked down at the flowing blood. A stain as red as his own was against the girl's cheek.

In Shilha, the Lieutenant said, "Come with me."

She withdrew a little farther, head erect, glaring, drawing the cloak the auctioneer had handed her tightly about her white body.

The Lieutenant knew he was acting a fool. The girl hated him and, suddenly, he hated the girl.

In a voice as hard as Toledo steel, he said, "Come with me or stay where you are. I care very little what you do. I bought you with no intention of giving you anything but your liberty. You can stay here and be damned!"

He about-faced, started down. The crowd opened a path for him.

Heels ringing on the stones, he went across the square and turned down a side street, heading back for the fort.

He stopped and looked back.

The girl was ten feet behind him and they were, for the moment, alone.

Nothing had altered in her manner. She was merely following him because she could do nothing else.

"Walk beside me, if you'll walk at all," said the Lieutenant, harshly.

13

"Slaves," she said, "always follow at a respectful distance." Her voice purred in a deadly way. "Lead on, my master."

The Lieutenant twisted at his crop as though half minded to beat her with it. But he turned and went toward the tall gates of the fort.

Two Legionnaires on sentry go saluted smartly, faced outward and blocked the girl with naked bayonets crossed before her.

"*Allez-vous-en,*" said Private Schmaltz.

"Beat it," added Private John Smith.

Her eyes passed over their faces and swept back again, hard enough to leave a wide red path. In French, she said, "Stand aside, camels."

The sentries faltered. They glanced at the Lieutenant, now some paces within the gate.

"Let her through!"

"*Oui, mon Lieutenant,*" said Private Schmaltz, blinking his small red eyes offendedly at the tone.

The men in the compound stopped as though they had been playing statues. Without looking to the right or left, the girl, barefooted but regal in the tightly held djellaba, followed the Lieutenant up the steps to his quarters.

He stood there, waiting for her.

"Go in," he said, coldly.

She stepped into the dim room, went straight across it and stood looking out of a port in the opposite wall.

The Lieutenant motioned toward his orderly room. "On the other side of that you'll find a spare bunk. You will not be disturbed."

She turned and faced him. "You do not look like a man to be afraid, *mon Lieutenant*. I am, after all, quite at your mercy. I realize that I am bought like a bale of rough cotton. I am quite ready to act my part."

"I will send you home at the first opportunity, *demoiselle*," said the Lieutenant.

"I cannot go home, *mon Lieutenant*. They would kill me to save the honor of the house for fear of what might have happened after the raid. That nothing happened will affect them not at all. I would die, regardless. I am, as I have said, your slave. Do with me as you will. I belong to you. I am owned. Brain, body and my soul, if I had one, are yours."

As she spoke her head came farther back. A faint flush was on her face. Her hand shook a little as it held the cape. But the tremor came from anger. She was mocking him.

The Lieutenant turned smartly to his desk, drew back the chair and seated himself. He picked up a sheaf of papers as though about to work on them.

"I suppose," she said, "I am dismissed?"

The Lieutenant lifted his head. His nostrils were thin and quivering with rage. His mouth was a black slit through which gleamed clenched teeth.

"This much has happened. I have made a fool of myself in the market, and I must make prestige take the place of the men and guns I do not have. I have accepted six or seven hundred pieces of gold from a Jew, whose purposes I do not know, to pay for you. If I do anything about restoring you to the Jeppas, I make the Harj people my enemies. If I keep you, I make the Jeppas my enemies. If I use you as a slave, I lose the respect of my men because I fraternize with a native woman and will not let them. If I billet you in town, they will think I visit you there. Now, do you see what I've done?"

She picked a cigarette out of a silver box on his desk. She applied a match to it, inhaled the smoke and blew it contemptuously at his face.

"It seems," she said bitterly, "that I am something of a problem, *mon Lieutenant*. I little reckoned that the fate of men and nations would rest so heavily upon my frail shoulders. Lieutenant, suppose we were to make the best of this. You own me. You cannot get rid of me because you say you cannot. You cannot marry me because a man cannot marry a slave." Her eyes grew thin and green. "Suppose you keep me. You are handsome. Better than any Berber or Arab. Has anyone ever told you, *mon Lieutenant*, that you have the face of a devil, and a very handsome devil too? Hah, you look like *Shaitan* when you smile like that, *mon Lieutenant*. Your eyes are beautiful when they are hard with anger. Perhaps, *mon Lieutenant*, I could love you." She shrugged and her beautiful mouth curved down. "And perhaps not. Perhaps I shall kill you, and again, perhaps not. Perhaps you will love me and never let me go. I am beautiful. I have been taught that. It is all I know, this beauty. Ah, but then, you will cast it aside and leave it to little use. Sell me again, Lieutenant. There are buyers. Sell me to that gross fool with the jiggling belly who bid the two hundred pieces of gold. Not enough, *mon Lieutenant*. I am worth more than that. But no. No, perhaps you are French and the French . . . but no, you cannot be French. English?"

"American," said the Lieutenant. "And Americans are

barbarians who know nothing about chivalry. Your name was Morgiana, was it not? A descendant of that pleasant lady who poured the boiling oil upon Ali Baba's robbers and who stabbed the robber chief with a poniard?"

"Perhaps," said the girl. "And perhaps not. Come, *mon Lieutenant*, I care nothing for a name and you care nothing. Why, you have bought me! I am as much your furniture as that chair in which you are sitting, and I should be quite as nameless."

He stared at her, still fascinated by her beauty and with her reckless, headstrong, untamed manner.

She leaned across the desk toward him until her face was not a foot from his.

Involuntarily he started to kiss her lips, hypnotized by her.

She straightened and her mouth was twisted down again. Slowly her fingers closed over the haft of a miniature dress sword the Lieutenant employed in the opening of letters.

She tested the sharp blade, smiled and backed away.

"Morgiana tried her steel with a bandit. I may try mine with a lieutenant." She gave him a small, mocking bow. "Your trusted, worshiping slave."

Regally she gathered her djellaba about her, crossed the orderly room and closed the door of the chamber he had designated.

The Lieutenant heard the key grate in the lock.

For hours he sat where he was, staring down at the arch of wounds she had given his hand. When he clenched his fist until the knuckles paled, small rubies of blood welled out and dropped, one by one, to his desk.

17

*"Morgiana tried her steel with a bandit.
I may try mine with a lieutenant."*

CHAPTER TWO

And Trouble Gathers

THE next morning the Lieutenant was having his coffee and a cigarette when Germaine brought him a sealed note. "A Berber just left it at the gate, sir," said Germaine. The Lieutenant ripped it open and read:

Commandant of Harj:

You are requested to come with the bearer of this message to take coffee with me at ten o'clock, or at your own convenience.

> Your servant in all Allah wills,
> Perviz al Bahman
> Caid

"Is the man waiting?" said the Lieutenant.

"Yes . . . er . . . I couldn't help but read the note upside down, *mon Lieutenant* . . . and . . . well, I served through the Rif campaign and I know this Perviz al Bahman. He runs mostly to fat and devilment and—"

"I'll go see him," said the Lieutenant.

"I'll turn you out a guard," said Germaine, scratching his brown beard. "There isn't any sense going to see that guy alone. He's worse than a whole town full of Berbers. If you'll pardon me, sir, I might add that it's probably about this woman you brought home last night—"

"Yes?"

"Well . . . don't look at me like that, Lieutenant. After all, we're in this pit together and the men are talking. They say the Jeppa will come down and wipe us out if Perviz al Bahman doesn't. I was thinking maybe if the Lieutenant wanted me to—"

"What?"

"I could sell her to somebody else for you. I had five offers this morning."

"Five?"

"She's a very beautiful woman, *mon Lieutenant,* and you could make yourself a purse full of money if you wanted to, no matter how much you paid for her. They said this morning that the reason nobody else bid was because you bid, and they think you realize by now that it'd be safer for all concerned if you were to sell her again quick. I think—"

"Thinking again?"

"Well, no, sir, but it is kind of a mess. We're on a frying pan. We couldn't hold this place for three days against this town and if Perviz al Bahman takes it into his head that he wants this woman—"

"I'm going down and see him about it."

"I'll go along."

"You'll stay here."

The sergeant raised his thick palms as though he wanted the good God to witness this folly. "*Mon Lieutenant!* This Perviz al Bahman will think nothing of killing you. Poison in your cup. A shot from the brush in his garden, a sudden assault against this fort, and there he'll have this woman and we'll all be too dead to do anything at all about it. Is your life worth nothing to you?"

"Not much," said the Lieutenant, beginning to dress.

"But it is to me!" wailed Germaine. "*Mon Lieutenant,* did you not save me once from the Tuaregs? Did I not once lead an assault column which saved you? Have I not lied for you time and again? *Mon Dieu,* I have some right to ask you to stay alive. Without you we would be butchered like so many sheep!"

"Sergeant," said the Lieutenant, buttoning his shirt, "I'm a fool. You know that. I have laid us open to attack from the Jeppa, from the town. But by God, I'm not going to see a lot of rotten Berbers sell this girl like they'd sell a hog."

"Madness," said the sergeant. "Madness."

The Lieutenant went down to the gate, saluted the Berber who waited there for him, and followed the man through the winding streets of the town.

They came, at length, to a high wall which continued the length of the street. The Lieutenant went through a small red door and found himself in a garden.

A fountain was splashing brightly amid clusters of tropical flowers. The place smelled sweetly of blossoms and incense. It was cool and restful, shutting out with palm fronds the heat of the morning.

In a marble pavilion, seated upon a cushion with yellow tassels, was Perviz al Bahman, robed for a state occasion, turbaned with silk.

He looked, in spite of his glorious clothing, like someone

had carved him from melting lard. His jowls sagged. His brows sagged. His stomach sagged over his crossed legs. He looked very tired, very sad, but he rose to greet the Lieutenant.

"The blessings of Allah upon you," said Perviz al Bahman.

"May Paradise await you," said the Lieutenant, politely.

"May music and children lighten your age."

"May the houris sing to you an eternity."

"May your coffers be ever overflowing," said the caid.

"May Allah recognize your nobility," said the Lieutenant.

"May your conquests of heart and sword be pleasant and many," said Perviz al Bahman. "Please sit down."

The Lieutenant laid kepi and crop aside and sat upon a cushion. A silent-footed girl came with a sherbet, paper-thin cups rimmed with gold, and cigarettes of an expensive kind for the Lieutenant. As silently, she went away.

Perviz al Bahman lifted his great head and then let it sag again. Woe was deep in his heart, it could be plainly seen, but he made a brave effort to be casual and hospitable.

"You find the city to your liking?"

"Beautiful," said the Lieutenant.

"It is a nice city," said Perviz, quite as though he had built it with his own hands. "I was surprised that the French do . . . that the French so long held off from it and now I am surprised that they garrison it with such a—begging your pardon, Commandant—such a small garrison."

"You are not on the main trade routes and the place is almost inaccessible from the North Coast," said the Lieutenant. "Perhaps, later, there will be roads built but that will take a long, long while. Perhaps, if things are peaceful"—he looked carefully at the caid—"the garrison may ever be small. The revenue to be realized here is very good, but the produce, due to the lack of roads, is destined only for local consumption. There will be no grain for France from here for many, many years. You are fortunate, Caid Perviz al Bahman, that you have so long remained secluded. You are doubly fortunate that you have the hill people and the desert people with whom to trade. Outside commerce is scarcely necessary to your prosperity."

"I am happy to hear you say that, Commandant."

"I am happy that you are so agreeable, sir. It would be inconvenient," said the Lieutenant without a trace of a smile, "if the regiments had to cross these mountains again and . . . well . . . perhaps change caids here."

Caid Perviz al Bahman nodded sadly. "Then, Commandant, we agree. You are a patrol, no more, no less. I served with the Riffs. I understand military purposes. You wish to send out a certain amount of gold to your government. I shall see to it that you have the gold to send. Further, I shall see to it that you yourself have . . ."

The Lieutenant's eyes were dangerous. He set down his cup very carefully, afraid that it would break in his tightening hands.

"Caid," said the Lieutenant, "I am not the conqueror. I am a soldier, a mercenary soldier, if you please, of the government of France. I find that my pay is ample."

"Ah, no, no, you do not understand me, Commandant. I

will pave your way for you. I will keep you here and keep your men safe. . . ."

"You are not to my taste with your words," said the Lieutenant.

"Pardon. Ah, a thousand pardons. You are brave and honorable and handsome. You are hot-tempered and impulsive and young. Good! What I would not give to have you in my service, Commandant! But you must have money. You must buy a great Arabian horse. You must fix your fort the better. You must see to it that your men can *buy* what they wish. Your coming gives me security, and to avoid the disturbances usually occasioned by foreign troops, the city will pay. And there is something else, Commandant."

Caid Perviz al Bahman wept a little. His wobbly head drooped upon his padded chest. His paunch heaved uneasily up and down against his knees. He was very sad.

"Already, Commandant, I am troubled. Yesterday in the public market you bought a certain woman. One named Morgiana Buddir al Buddor. Ah, you do not know how sleepless I have been since then. Ah, no, no, do not misunderstand. My sleeplessness was purely political, though she is undoubtedly the most heavenly woman in all *le Maroc*. Ah, I envy you, her eyes, her sweet cruel mouth, her milky shoulders and the flowing flame of gold which is her silken hair. But it was not that, Commandant."

"Caid, I am happy to know that it was not."

Something in the drawn-steel voice made the caid blink. But very soon he was sad again.

"There was a great mistake, Commandant. A *great* mistake.

This Morgiana, this jewel of the gods, is skilled in the arts of war. She is a virgin knight of the Jeppa. She rode a white, fire-breathing stallion and her cloak was of white-hot flame.

"In a slight skirmish with the Jeppa, we managed to cut off some of their baggage train, their camp. And in it were these women. As is customary, these women were to be sold here in the market as the Jeppa sell our women in their market. No matter. It is a fair exchange, lending a little excitement to a dull life. The women, usually, mind very little because we of Harj are *men*.

"But this one time, Commandant, my captain made a mistake. This Morgiana had been ill in camp. Without her cloak and stallion no one knew her. She said nothing, thinking it fatal to resist such overpowering numbers.

"We had no clue until my vizier heard her announce her own name in the public market. He was without money and he came running to get me. When we returned she was sold!

"You, Commandant, had bought her."

The caid fell silent, moving back and forth, grieving, eyes dropped to his stomach.

At last he said, "Commandant, may I ask that you give this woman up? May I ask that you accept twice your price for her? If you do not, matters will be very, very difficult. We cannot possibly keep her here in Harj."

The Lieutenant remained still.

"Commandant, you do not know these hill people. They are in separate clans and they fight one another. But when they have a great enough common cause they band together and then . . . then Harj is sacked." He suppressed a sob.

"We must give her back to them with all despatch. Ordinary women . . . well, that is merely sport. But this is horrible!"

"If I give her back to her own people," said the Lieutenant, "by her own confession she will die."

"Certainly! Or she will be made to kill herself. The Jeppa have nothing to do with those women who have been brought here. Long ago it began and . . . well, it is the custom, even with a woman such as Morgiana. But what is that, Commandant? What is that beside the lives of hundreds? Perhaps thousands? Should not that one die who causes this trouble? Give her up to me, Commandant."

The Lieutenant finished his coffee. He gathered his kepi and crop and stood up. He gave Perviz al Bahman a precise salute and bow.

"Noble caid," said the Lieutenant, "this Morgiana is no less a problem to me than she is to you. But I cannot allow her to be killed or mistreated. Good day."

Perviz al Bahman sighed deeply, and when he exhaled his whole body shook sadly.

"Nur," he said. "*Ai*, Nur ed Deen. Go ahead."

The Lieutenant saw a bush move at the side of the pavilion. A wrinkled, parched old man stepped out. He was holding an Italian pistol and the muzzle was centered on the Lieutenant's chest.

"Now?" said Nur ed Deen.

"Of course," groaned Perviz al Bahman.

Nur ed Deen cocked the weapon.

There was no cover closer than twelve feet. He had no side arms. And Nur ed Deen was about to drill the Lieutenant.

"Wait!" said the Lieutenant, bowing to Nur ed Deen. "You have no idea what would happen if you did this."

"Oh, yes," said Perviz al Bahman. "Of course. But it is necessary. Fire, Nur."

"The big mountain gun at the fort," said the Lieutenant, momentarily expecting the impact of a soft-nosed slug, "is trained on this garden. If I am not back within the hour, my sergeant has orders to blast your house, which is well within range."

"A pity," said Perviz al Bahman. "It is a good house, and after we shoot you we shall have to abandon it, I suppose. Besides, you left no such order. Well, Nur, go ahead."

Nur ed Deen raised the muzzle a little and sighted along it. "A pity to kill a man so young, my caid, but . . ."

His finger came down on the trigger.

An explosion racked the garden.

The Lieutenant had been so sure of the bullet that he stumbled back, convinced that he was hit.

An instant later he knew he was not.

Nur ed Deen collapsed slowly. The silver pistol fell from his hand. His head bent forward. His chest caved in. Limp, he hit the side of the pavilion with a soft thump.

Perviz al Bahman was very agile. He went backward as though shot from a catapult. He went over the edge of the pavilion and out of sight in an instant.

The Lieutenant wheeled and looked up at the wall.

Sergeant Germaine was there, head and hand and revolver in sight.

"Shall I shoot the other one?" said the sergeant.

The Lieutenant laughed. He strode rapidly toward the door in the wall.

Out of the house came three Berbers, alarmed at the sound of the shot, ready to defend their caid with their lives.

One of them had a rifle and he dropped to his knee to line the sights on the Lieutenant.

Sergeant Germaine fired and dropped the Berber over his gun.

The Lieutenant reached the door and dived through. Close behind him the other two men were yelling shrilly, waving swords and crying for blood.

The sergeant fired again and the first one dropped, the other hesitated for an instant.

In that instant the Lieutenant was gone.

The Lieutenant joined the sergeant in the street. They took to their heels, headed for alleys away from the main part of town and ran swiftly toward the fort.

"Perviz was too quick for me. I should have shot him first but I was afraid that guy Nur would beat me to it with you."

"What the hell were you doing there?" panted the Lieutenant as they turned a corner.

"I knew his reputation," said the sergeant. "I had fits when I saw you drinking his coffee."

"You were supposed to stay in the fort."

"But I knew—"

"When we get out of this you get five days' bread and water."

"*Oui, mon Lieutenant.* There'll be hell to pay after this and I'm not worried about seeing a nice, safe jail."

"Then I'll break you now."

"Who else would be a sergeant?"

"Run, damn you, and stop talking. There's the fort."

They slowed up and walked through the gate. The Lieutenant gave a series of staccato orders.

Lebels rattled. Hotchkiss guns were uncovered and mounted. The guard was tripled and the gate was closed and barred.

"Alert," said the Lieutenant. "They may attack after dark."

"Oui, mon Lieutenant," said the sergeant.

The Lieutenant went wearily up to his quarters, wondering how many days they could hold the place. Not more than a week at best, and no chance to get word to the main command.

"Women!" he said, harshly. "Devils!"

CHAPTER THREE

The Rising Horde

WHEN the first streaks of pearl crowned the Atlas, Perviz al Bahman began his attack. A scattering of rifle fire stabbed long strings of orange sparks into the gray red morning. Bullets churned rock splinters from the battlements.

Across from the fort was a long street of flat-topped houses. Perviz al Bahman's warriors had taken these, silently barricading them with sandbags after the fashion some of the elders had learned in the long-past Riff wars.

It sounded as though some small boy had set off a package of firecrackers. Then there was silence.

The Lieutenant mounted the battlement and strode along behind the embrasures. His Legionnaires were keeping down, showing no more than their front sights to the enemy.

It was still much too dark to see distinct targets and the orders were to hold fire until an attack was made on the gate. Shooting from those low roofs, the Berbers and Arabs could not hope to hit much.

The Lieutenant wondered fitfully if Jean Patou had gotten through. Ah, well, no matter, help could not possibly arrive for a week even under forced marches.

Down the street which led up to the main gate, the Lieutenant could see a cluster of white. Men were gathering there and as the light became brighter, it could be seen that they had a long battering ram. They were approaching at a walk.

The Lieutenant touched the shoulder of a machine gunner.

"*Attendre, mon enfant.* Prepare to rake that rabble, but do not pull until they are within a hundred feet of the gate."

"*Oui, mon Lieutenant.*"

The Lieutenant went on down the battlement. He touched the men in the embrasures one by one.

"Take the first on the right, Raussman. . . . Second on the right, Fourelle . . . Third on the right, Dijou . . . First on the left, Ritter . . . Second on the left, *caporal* . . . Third on the left, Renault . . ."

The group came steadily on. A scattering burst of fire rapped out from the houses. Smoke rolled like mist, curling with the breeze. Mausers, Mannlichers, Sniders, even Lebels, were out there, each different in sound. Steel-jacketed slugs and soft-nosed bullets chewed great gashes out of the embrasures. Lead whined and screamed as it ricocheted.

The Legionnaires kept down. The Lieutenant was exposed each time he passed an embrasure, but he did not duck. They knew him out there by his cap. It would have been wiser to have thrown the cap away and used a common kepi.

Each time the men on the roofs caught a glimpse of the Lieutenant's red, gold and blue headgear, a volley would crash out and lead sang like a smashed harp all about the Lieutenant's body.

The group with the battering ram came on. They were

trotting now, encouraged by the fact that no fire had come from the fort. They were gray as smoke.

"Steady. We'll see a lot of this, Gervaise," said the Lieutenant. "Sergeant, how many do you suppose there are out there?"

"Enough," said Germaine.

"Quite," said the Lieutenant.

"Maybe two thousand," said the sergeant.

"Odds only thirty-three to one?" said the Lieutenant. "Well, well, Sergeant, I thought this might be serious."

Legionnaire Schmaltz, a little ferret-faced man, gave a nervous, pipsqueak laugh, making certain his Lebel was at full cock. Schmaltz was shaking with excitement. He had a bad reputation because he invariably shot for the abdomen and then crowed over the antics of his victim as the poor devil writhed in agony.

"Where do you suppose Perviz al Boogeyman is?" said Germaine, thoughtfully picking his teeth with a brass clip.

"Him? He hasn't left his harem yet," said the Lieutenant.

The group before the gate narrowed their distance to a hundred and fifty feet. They were running now, heading their ram for the gate.

The Lieutenant glanced at his watch, said, "Huh, only five-thirty and I'm hungry and no breakfast until six. Sergeant, go down and stir up that cook and tell him I want a good cup of coffee. All right, Legionnaires. Ready. Aim. Fire!"

Like the single beat of a gigantic drum, a score of Lebels barked through the embrasures.

The Hotchkiss machine gun set up a high, cackling laughter. Stopped.

The group in gray djellabas, carried forward by their own speed, pitched into the dirt and skidded to a limp, sloppy stop. The battering ram, its momentum greater, plowed a twenty-foot furrow in the dirt.

An angry, crackling volley fire came from the roofs of the houses. Hundreds of rounds slapped and screamed against the stone battlements, seeking hot and bloody vengeance for the wholesale slaughter of the assault party.

But the Legionnaires were down and out of sight.

Germaine came up with a cup of coffee for the Lieutenant.

"Cooky says if one of you gents will crawl down and get those stiffs," said Germaine, pointing, "he'll serve you Harj stew for breakfast."

The Lieutenant sat on an ammunition case and sipped his coffee, looking up at the Atlas sunrise as though it was the only thing to be seen in the whole landscape.

"Another assault party!" yelped Raussman.

"Tell them to wait until I've finished," said the Lieutenant, remaining where he was. "How many?"

"About thirty!"

"Take the numbers I gave you before. How close are they?"

"About three hundred yards."

The Lieutenant swung his booted leg, lighted a cigarette and resumed his study of the sunrise. He could hear the jingle of swords and the slap of running feet outside the wall.

"Fifty yards!" sang out Raussman.

"Ready, range twenty-five yards," said the Lieutenant.

"Look at that coloring, Sergeant. Isn't it marvelous? I ought to get up earlier. Makes you feel peppy. Aim. Fire!"

Another mighty clap of thunder. A clattering encore from the Hotchkiss.

"Missed," wept Schmaltz. "I hit him in the neck."

A rattling roll of musketry battered the fort again. The Berbers and Arabs on the houses jumped up and shot standing in their rage.

"Lieutenant?" said Piccard, the machine gunner.

"At will," said the Lieutenant.

The Hotchkiss rattled and coughed and writhed, churning brown dust from the sandbagged roofs. Berbers went over the edge and down like dropped bombs.

The Lieutenant stood up and stretched. "First, second and third squads go below for breakfast. The rest of you keep down. Raussman, watch the street. Sergeant, take over."

He walked down the battlement to the stairs and then down the runway to his quarters.

Morgiana was there. Her face was ivory white and her eyes were hot and excited.

"How many of the fools are there?" said Morgiana.

The Lieutenant sat down at his desk, lighted a cigarette and flipped the match into an ashtray. "A few."

"You mean a thousand or more. Perviz al Bahman can muster three thousand fighting men if he chooses. That's fifty to one. What are you going to do?"

"Knock them down every time they come up. You start worrying when I start."

She lifted her head proudly. "Time enough to worry when

there's nothing else to be done, *mon Lieutenant.* Where are they concentrated?"

"On the town side."

"Had you thought to post a sentry on this side?"

"Oh, yes," said the Lieutenant.

"Your attack will come from there unless I have spent my time knitting instead of fighting this same swine. If you have food and water for a month, you might still hold out. Would your superiors know about this?"

"Perhaps."

"You sent a man?"

"Jean Patou. He's good at that sort of thing. He went by the upper pass."

"Then he never got through," said Morgiana. "The Jeppas have started to patrol there and he is certain to be picked up."

"Poor Jean."

"The Jeppas have no love for Legionnaires since this thing has happened to me," said Morgiana. "You will have to stand them off and hope for the best."

"Ah, well, what the hell," said the Lieutenant.

She looked strangely at him. There was something different about him which she had not noticed before. Since the Harj warriors had attacked, the Lieutenant had changed his whole personality. He actually looked happy.

Before this he had been irritable and worried. He had been gruff and abrupt. But now he was breezy and jaunty. His kepi was over his eye, and he had bright lights in his eyes and he wore a wide, pleased grin.

Suddenly she understood him. He was a man of action,

wholly and completely. The cares and worries of state were irksome to him. He asked no more from life than a chance to try his metal and his wits with an antagonist worthy of him.

With a panicky feeling, she thought that he did not realize the danger he faced. It annoyed her that he should take the lives of his men and herself so lightly.

"Perhaps," said Morgiana, "my lord and master thinks this is a chess game without any serious consequences. I have seen this Perviz al Bahman fight. He will never grant an honorable surrender to anyone who has offended him. It is his special delight to butcher any opposing force to the man. He has you penned like so many hogs in a corral and he will give you as little mercy as though you would be pork for his dinner. I have seen him fight. He is cunning and ruthless. Out there he has three thousand warriors. In here you have sixty men. The odds are fifty to one against your getting away from here alive. If you retreat into the hills, the Jeppas will slaughter you. If you stay, you will soon exhaust your stores of food and water and be compelled to surrender or starve to death."

"Ah, yes, my pretty slave and handmaiden. . . ." She winced because he had never said that before. He was stealing her attitude and her lines. He was turning her own process of annihilation against her. "I quite realize that Perviz al Bahman is not a playmate to be despised. My good Sergeant Germaine shot down Nur ed Deen, his vizier, and two captains of his guard. I have here a woman he would sell his soul to own. I am a part of an army which conquered and humbled him. But," he snapped his fingers, "this battle is not yet done, my beautiful black-eyed houri."

"He will batter down your gate and an avalanche of steel will flow through in spite of your guns. You can do nothing against that."

"As for his gate, you heard that Lebel volley a moment ago? You heard that machine-gun rattle? He tried again and failed. Those attacks are nothing. He is preparing to ladder the walls on this side and scale us. I have kegs of grenades waiting for him there. Did you ever see what a grenade will do to a ladder full of men? Very, very effective, little serf."

His confidence when he must know that there was no way out had a queer effect upon her. Was he trying to keep her from worrying or did he actually believe in himself to that extent?

"You're either a fool or a hero," said Morgiana.

"There is no difference there, sweet morsel. To become a hero a man must first become a fool. All I lack is my cap and bells and pig's bladder. Ah, there they go. Another attack coming. I must call the men up from breakfast. Odd that they have so many guns."

"They brought them south when they refused to surrender to the Spanish in the Rif. They know how to use them, *mon Lieutenant.*"

"Oh, yes. No doubt. By the way, where is our friend Ibn Batuta?"

She looked steadily at him, trying to read his eyes. "Why do you ask me that?"

He grinned at her. "Everything is beginning to work just as he wanted it to. Here I am, sewed up in a fort, there is Perviz al Bahman about to have all hell shot out of him. Do you know a pawn when you see one?"

"Chess was invented by the Arabs," she retorted.

"There is a question about that. However, my dear little hostage, a pawn, when moved all the way up the board to the opponent's own king row, becomes anything its owner wants it to become. I choose to become the most powerful piece on the board. Just how, I leave it to the gods to decide. This is not the first time I've been penned up, as you say, like so many pigs."

His gay, nonchalant manner was eating into her. Did something lie behind his words? He had called her a hostage. Did he know? Would he actually win out against Perviz al Bahman? Did he already suspect that all this was a tangled spider web of intrigue?

She had, so far, taken him for the average officer. Brave, gallant, but not exactly endowed with genius. But he was an American. And Americans, she had reason to know, were a queer breed, half mad, reckless, daring anything, playing for stakes higher than a European could conceive.

The man, she knew with a shock, was an unreadable mystery. She did not know his name, why he was there, what he was doing in a French Foreign Legion uniform or anything at all about him except that he was, for the moment, her owner—a fact which bit into her like acid, no matter the part she had played in determining it.

Tall, graceful, so cheerful that it was gruesome to see him grin, the Lieutenant went out into the bright sunlight of morning.

"On the battlements!" he shouted to his men who had been eating below.

They streamed up the steps, wiping their mouths, adjusting their cartridge belts, gripping their Lebels as holy men hang on to their souls. A hellbent crew, forsaken by the world, given up by their families, cast like rolling dice into the sun-hammered rawness of Africa to kill and be killed for an empire they neither owned nor respected.

The Lieutenant sought out Germaine. The sergeant was thoughtfully walking up and down, still picking his teeth abstractedly.

"Any luck?" said the Lieutenant.

"Twenty more in the last assault party. If we keep this up, they'll get sick to their bellies of us and go off and leave us alone."

"Sure. Sure, they'll walk right off just like that. By the way, have we got enough ammunition for the mountain gun?"

"All depends upon what you want to do with it, sir."

"Oh, I thought we might try knocking the caid's house to pieces as a starter and then we'll begin on the mosques, and when there are no more minarets, we might start on the markets, and then when they're pounded into rock dust we'll begin on the houses of the prominent chiefs. And if they still think they want to besiege us, we'll fire phosphorus shells over and burn their town around their ears."

"Oh, I guess we've got enough for that," said the sergeant. "That's the caid's dump with the blue roof, isn't it? All right. Redman! You and Svenson and Norcroft lug up the cases for the mountain gun. Piccard, man the sights. The caid's house and then the mosques and then the markets and then the other houses, you said?"

"That's right. Give me a corporal and four men. I'm going to wait for an assault on the north side."

"On the north side! Huh, that's why the firing is getting stiffer here."

"I wish," said the Lieutenant, wistfully, "that we had some tubs of Greek fire and some boiling oil and such. It isn't as dangerous as grenades, but it certainly looks impressive."

"Think we'll get out of here?" said Germaine.

"Who knows?" said the Lieutenant. "And outside of the girl, who the hell cares? You've lived too long already. So have I. If we win, the whole thing will be forgotten. If we lose, we'll take plenty of them with us to carry our packs down under. Harj won't forget this scrap right away. By the way, did you know we were fighting for the Jeppas?"

"No!" cried the sergeant, jolted out of his calm.

"Yep," said the Lieutenant.

The Lieutenant moved along the battlement toward the north, but as he went he stopped occasionally to touch a shoulder and speak a word of caution, praise or encouragement.

He hefted a Legionnaire's bandolier. "Getting light. How many have you killed?"

Gregoff, the Legionnaire, blinked and confessed to only two. "But one was sniping over there," he added.

"Ah, *non, non,*" said the Lieutenant. "So many bullets for only two men? What are we? Spahis? Look, my dirty-faced little cabbage, let me have that Lebel. These cartridges are expensive! They cost, every one, almost as much as you make in a week. So you see, Papa *Presidente* would be very angry. He could do without you easily, but the money for cartridges? *Non!*"

41

The Lieutenant leaned through the embrasure. Across the roofs he could see a man who was changing positions. He set the sights with a flip of his finger, leaned his elbow against the rock, fired.

The warrior stopped in midair, slumped down into a dirty gray heap and lay still. A hand snaked out to get his ammunition belt. The Lieutenant fired again and the second Berber dropped into sight. A sniper showed his head, trying to see where the shots were coming from and the Lieutenant fired a third time, accurately.

"See? You pin their headcloths on tight so that they will not lose them," said the Lieutenant. "Now, you have perhaps a hundred bullets left. When I return I shall expect you to show me the carcasses of a hundred men. See?"

"Oui, mon Lieutenant," said Gregoff, grinning and taking back his rifle.

The Lieutenant moved on. When he passed embrasures, Harj slugs yapped about him like shrapnel. He did not duck because, if he ducked, it would be too late anyway.

Ahead of him, a Legionnaire screamed and dropped back from his post, dropping his rifle and clutching his face. A ricochet from the slot in the wall had torn away half his cheek and four of his teeth.

He recovered himself and spat out fragments of ivory and flesh. He picked up his rifle, jabbed it through the slot, sighted along it and squeezed carefully. The recoil jolted him. He withdrew the gun, saying, "That'll keep him awhile," and sat down on an ammunition case to bandage his face.

Acrid powder fumes curled along the battlement. The

air was churned with maimed slugs. From time to time the Hotchkiss gun on the north side leaped and barked like an excited hound pack as it mowed down sallies made by the warriors toward a tree clump on the hillside.

The Lieutenant stopped. "What's happening?"

"Concentration there," said the gunner. "If we had a mountain gun on the spot—"

"It's busy," said the Lieutenant, pointing in the direction of its bass-drum banging. "Can't you rake those trees?"

"I tried, but it's a waste of bullets, *mon Lieutenant*."

"Then stop shooting altogether, Corporal. Here, Legionnaires, cease firing."

The men all along the north wall—which had about a dozen embrasures—stepped back from their posts and looked questioningly at the Lieutenant.

"Stop shooting them," said the Lieutenant. "One bullet apiece is too much to pay. Cease firing until I give the order. Pick up those grenades, pile them at your feet and wait."

"They've been fixing ladders, sir."

"Fine," said the Lieutenant.

"They'll try to put them up on the wall in a minute, sir."

"Fine," said the Lieutenant. "Let them. Have you a cigarette, Jehan?"

The Legionnaire addressed pulled forth a sweaty pack and offered one. The Hotchkiss gunner handed over a match. The Lieutenant took a long drag, leaned against the parapet and began to hum thoughtfully.

"Jehan," he said, presently, "if you had a million francs, what would you do with it?"

43

"I'd get drunk," said Jehan, promptly.

"I was afraid of that."

The Hotchkiss gunner fingered his grip and shifted restlessly upon his tripod seat. "They're bringing out the ladders and running toward the wall, sir."

"Oh yes, so they are. Well, let them put them up."

"Yes, sir."

"If I had a million dollars, Jehan, you know what I would do?"

"No, *mon Lieutenant.*"

"I'd get drunk. Have they got the ladders up yet?"

"Almost," said the Hotchkiss gunner, nervously.

"See the ground this side of those trees?" said the Lieutenant. "When I give the word, start fanning it. Plow it up as though you wanted to plant some wild oats."

"Oui, mon Lieutenant."

"The rest of you pick up grenades. Stand where those ladders rest, pull the pins and wait. My, how athletic they are."

About three hundred men poured out of the clump of trees and sprinted toward the place their advance had set ladders against the fort wall. Waving swords and revolvers and rifles, the horde threw itself at the seventy-five-foot ascent. Like apes in cloaks, they came swarming up the ladders until the whole side of the fort looked like a moving wall drapery.

Eyes white, teeth clenched, weapons jangling, they came swiftly up, ready to launch themselves with a will into the task of slaughtering every Legionnaire in the fort.

A silence prevailed for an instant. The leaders had reached the top.

"Grenades!" roared the Lieutenant.

From the embrasures, black shapes the size of baseballs dropped beside the ladders. Halfway down they exploded. Their shrapnel rattled against the fort, ripped and tore into the horde of men below.

"Hotchkiss!"

The machine gunner raked the designated patch of ground which the retreat would have to cross.

"Grenades!"

The plummeting shapes dropped again, exploded. Shreds of cloth dangled from the rungs. Here and there a wild-eyed, terrified warrior clung desperately, unable to go up or down.

The Lieutenant reached through and gripped the top of a ladder and gave it a mighty push backward. It stood up straight, hesitated as though about to walk away of its own accord and then, with the remnants of its human cargo still clinging, it swooped outward to jar the earth.

"Hotchkiss cease firing," called the Lieutenant.

The wall was quiet again. The Lieutenant picked up his cigarette from the parapet where he had carefully laid it down, puffed thoughtfully upon it as though making a momentous decision and said:

"Yes, I'd get drunk."

CHAPTER FOUR

Night Slashed with Firing

A T ten-thirty, the Lieutenant noticed a commotion at the opposite end of the battlement. He strode quickly in that direction, expecting from the looks of his Legionnaires that Perviz al Bahman was there in person.

But in this he was disappointed. Morgiana had decided that it was too dark and uncomfortable in his quarters and had started up the steps to the parapets.

The Lieutenant was at the top to meet her. "A lot of hornets buzzing around up here, *demoiselle*. You might get stung."

"If you expect me to remain below and have all the noise without any of the excitement, my lord and master, you are quite mistaken."

"You wouldn't, by any chance," said the Lieutenant, "want to signal anyone, would you?"

Again her eyes were unreadable and opaque. She did not know how much he knew and how much he was guessing at. She faltered and drew her pure white cape tightly about her.

He was standing up there, feet apart, kepi rakish, hands on his hips, riding crop jutting out at right angles, a cigarette dangling from his lips.

A gunner situated in a mosque some six hundred meters away from the fort was trying, and had been trying for the last three hours, to put a heavy, long-range bullet into the blue and

47

gold Lieutenant, but had not so far gotten closer than a good two feet.

Just now one of his bullets slapped rock beside the Lieutenant's right boot and went screaming off at an angle, directly over Morgiana's golden head.

Involuntarily she ducked. The Lieutenant laughed at her. "I thought you caught bullets in your teeth," said the Lieutenant.

Furious, she stood where she was. "I am not as big a fool as you are, *mon Lieutenant.*"

"When they snap like that," said the Lieutenant, "they're miles away by the time you dodge. Didn't you know that? I've been ducking all morning, but my neck got tired and so I quit. Want to come up and look around?"

Very little firing was being done from the fort. This was the first time most of the men had seen Morgiana. She was a momentary legend with them. Those who had caught a fleet glimpse of her through the Lieutenant's door had told the others what a looker she was, how lucky the Lieutenant was, and how they'd never seen such a woman.

Prepared, they thought, for anything, the Legionnaires were astounded by her appearance. She carried herself like a queen and she made them all feel inadequate and speechless.

The Lieutenant turned to his men on the battlement. "Fire at will, *mes enfants.* Make them keep their heads down."

The Lebels began to rap sharply. The Lieutenant beckoned to the girl to come up.

She showed no trace of fear. Calmly she walked the whole length of the runway, stopping now and then to look through an embrasure.

"Making sure they know you're here, eh?" said the Lieutenant. "All right. They've seen you, you can go below. But what's the next move? After all, my little delicacy, I am commandant of the garrison and I might want to know what tactics to use."

"Any tactics you like, my lord and master," she said sweetly. "You might stand up there in the tower and make faces at them. You would be an excellent target."

The men on the roofs were not shooting now. For one thing, the Lebels were ripping up sand from the native barricades, and for another, Morgiana could be seen from the lookouts.

Presently, seeing that their volleys were not needed, the Legionnaires ceased firing too. It was an uneasy silence which prevailed. The sounds of shots had echoed against the hills since dawn and now that everything was still, silence itself had a humming, heavy sound.

"Perviz al Bahman is running no chances of hitting you," said the Lieutenant. "I wish he were that considerate of me. There have been half a hundred snipers going about their business of trying to kill me all morning. Perhaps I should hide behind a woman's skirts, eh? And keep you walking here with me. By the way, have you ever seen such a view? Look at those mountains, now. Big and rugged and overpowering. And take that desert, for instance. Nothing has ever been as yellow as that is now. If you'd only stay I could be most entertaining."

"I'm certain you would be. Very amusing. By the way, my lord and master, have you figured your way out of this?"

"Oh, this?" said the Lieutenant, quite as if it all amounted to exactly nothing. "I'm a man of the moment, little slave. If the moment comes, we shall, I assure you, be saved. In the meantime, we've never had so many excellent targets at once, eh, Sergeant?"

"If you would wear a different cap," snorted Germaine, "you'll stop being a target."

"Ah, well, the penalty one has to pay for position. The higher your standing in society, the better target you are. And now, my dearest serf, if you will go below, we'll get on with this war. Your presence embarrasses the enemy."

"*Adieu, mon Lieutenant,*" said Morgiana, smiling and giving him her hand. "It has been a pleasure, hating you. Perhaps time will even up the score."

She went down to his quarters again and disappeared. Instantly came the discord of Mannlichers, Mausers, Lebels and Sniders.

Voice dulled by the din, Germaine said, "Sounded like she was taking a trip."

"Across the compound is the only place you can travel here. But, get on with it, Sergeant. Have you started on the mosques? No? Well, there's that one over there with the sniper in it. Knock it down."

"*Oui, mon Lieutenant.* With pleasure."

Through the heat of the day, the battle went on. The Legionnaires, taking good care not to expose themselves, suffered remarkably few and minor casualties.

When evening slowly came, the Lieutenant looked very tired. But nothing like weariness showed itself in his voice. Walking up and down, up and down, conserving the strength of his men at the expense of his own, he was cheerful and witty.

Many of these Legionnaires had served with him before and knew his way in a fight. Many were new to both fighting and the Lieutenant, but they began to appreciate both.

Only Germaine knew one horrible, nerve-racking fact. Only when his back was against the wall, only when his last bullet was ready to fire, only when water and provisions and all hope ran out, was the Lieutenant so gay.

The sergeant knew without asking that the Lieutenant never expected to get out of this fort alive. He knew that the situation was hopeless. That in three or four days they would begin to starve and weave back and forth. Men would have to be propped up in the embrasures, dead and the living together, to make certain that the warriors would think they still had a fighting complement left.

There would be dead Legionnaires on the morrow. With a long black night ahead, Perviz al Bahman had all manner of devilment arranged.

And with the coming of complete darkness, the Lieutenant's jokes and sallies grew better and better.

And the sergeant knew positively that not one man would ever get out of the fight with his head still on his shoulders. The Lieutenant would never be like that if it was not the truth.

Dolefully, the sergeant began to batter his third minaret with the mountain gun. The moon had been up in the daylight. It turned the world a blue silver now. As daylight had faded, the flame from gun muzzles had grown longer and longer, brighter and brighter, until now in the night a shot looked like the tail of a skyrocket. All along the battlements, the embrasures lit up at intermittent intervals. From the mountains it probably looked like a swarm of fireflies.

Legionnaires looked big and blurred against the flares of their own shots. The towers of the fort stood like black giants over everything.

The Lieutenant had had nothing to eat since noon and it was now eight. Schmaltz came to tell him that his dinner was ready.

The Lieutenant went down the steps to his quarters. He intended to have a shave and perhaps a bath. It would wake him up. Fresh linen and a clean body had a lot to do with morale. As soon as he had eaten he would rest and then dress.

He entered his office. The cook had set a tray on his desk and, on the tray, besides the dinner, was a tall bottle of cognac. It is always a mystery how cooks can hide such things until the proper moment to produce them.

Thinking that Morgiana might like a drink with him, he called to her. There was no answer.

"Guns deafened her, I guess," he muttered, going to her door and knocking upon it.

No answer.

"Morgiana!"

Still no answer.

He thrust the door open and looked into her dark room. He went back to his office and got a lamp and entered again.

Her clothes were there, lying in a fluffy white heap upon the rug. But Morgiana was nowhere to be seen.

STORIES from the GOLDEN AGE

☐ Yes, I would like to receive my **FREE CATALOG** featuring all 80 volumes of the *Stories from the Golden Age Collection* and more!

Name _____

Shipping Address _____

City _____ State _____ ZIP _____

Telephone _____ E-mail _____

Check other genres you are interested in: ☐ SciFi/Fantasy ☐ Western ☐ Mystery

FREE SHIPPING!
NO PURCHASE REQUIRED

6 Books • 8 Stories
Illustrations • Glossaries

6 Audiobooks • 12 CDs
8 Stories • Full color 40-page booklet

Fold on line and tape

IF YOU ENJOYED READING THIS BOOK, GET THE ACTION/ADVENTURE COLLECTION **AND** SAVE 25%

BOOK SET	**AUDIOBOOK SET**
~~$59.50~~ $45.00	~~$77.50~~ $58.00
ISBN: 978-1-61986-089-6	ISBN: 978-1-61986-090-2

☐ Check here if shipping address is same as billing.

Name _____

Billing Address _____

City _____ State _____ ZIP _____

Telephone _____ E-mail _____

Credit/Debit Card #: _____

Card ID # (last 3 or 4 digits): _____

Exp Date: _____/_____ Date (month/day/year): _____/_____/_____

Order Total *(CA and FL residents add sales tax)*: _____

To order online, go to: **www.GoldenAgeStories.com** or call toll-free **1-877-8GALAXY** or 1-323-466-7815

He walked quickly to her bed and saw a note pinned to her pillow. It was written with a kohl stick in Arabic. It said, "*Adieu,* again, my gallant Lieutenant. I believe you have read through a gross deception. If I do not again see you on this earth, I shall meet you at the banquet table of the warriors in Paradise. Your devoted slave, Morgiana."

Where she could have gone and why, he did not know. He ordered out a search party and ransacked the fort. He took a pair of night glasses and studied the lines about the building and knew that she could not have gotten through.

Had she given herself up to the caid, Perviz al Bahman, to save the fort?

No, that could not be. She hated him too thoroughly for that.

Then where had she gone and why? Where was she? At the mercy of the Jeppa who would kill her? At the headquarters of Perviz al Bahman? In the mountains? In the town?

She had come like a goddess; she was gone like a *jinnī.* Exotic, fiery, beautiful . . .

Standing in a tower, wind rippling his kepi cloth, field glasses to his eyes as he studied the town and the mountains, the Lieutenant began to doubt that she had ever existed at all.

Below him the rifle fire went on in brilliant, angry discord. Above him in the moonlight the gigantic Atlas were unperturbed and mysterious. Before him like a silver sea stretched the endless desert.

"My lord and master," breathed the Lieutenant with a weary smile. "I would to God she had really meant that. Then dying wouldn't be so hard to take. . . .

"Sergeant! Assault party on the south wall! Hotchkiss! Fire at will! Piccard, get me that sniper on the red roof!"

Tired, dragging hours of blackness. The moon was gone and the sun would come and another broiling day would begin. Fifty to one . . . well, he'd carve them down a little before they got him.

CHAPTER FIVE

The Lieutenant
Tries a Trick

T WO days filled with spitefully cracking rifle fire thundered their way into the past.

For two days, the Lieutenant held Perviz al Bahman at a stalemate. On the face, the attack looked hopeless.

But down in the storerooms, the shelved food began to show wide gaps and the water butts, one by one, were rolled aside, empty. In spite of all conservation of both water and rations, the Lieutenant knew that he did not have twenty-four hours left.

After that it would be a delirium of attack and repulse. Legionnaires would cling haggardly to the embrasures, faces drawn, tongues swelling until they could no longer yell, belts tightening to the last notch.

Food and water and ammunition. On these things depend the fate of armies. No amount of physical courage or wise strategy can offset their lack.

And on the chill dawning of the third day, when all the world was bathed in scarlet, the Lieutenant grew morose.

Sergeant Germaine, seeing it, cheered up. Again he took to joking with the men, beginning when the Lieutenant left off. The sergeant knew his officer. When things were hopeless, the Lieutenant was cheerful. When sighting some means of deliverance, the Lieutenant, in the labors of thought, drew into himself.

The warriors were growing bolder. This morning the sandbags on the roof were higher than they had been at sunset. Darting headcloths were more frequent, snipers more persistent.

Three Legionnaires were dead, eight were wounded. One Hotchkiss was out of action completely.

"Sergeant," said the Lieutenant as they leaned against the watchtower. "We must do something. I've exhausted my wits and I still see no answer. Perhaps you have an idea."

"If the Lieutenant hasn't, how could I?" said Germaine, thoughtfully removing imaginary specks from between his molars with a bayonet.

"Since Morgiana left, I've been trying to think of ways and means of doing two things. Sergeant, it amounts to this: We are getting tired. This incessant noise and the constant strain of being on the alert will make the men more careless. From now on we can count on more numerous and serious casualties."

"Oui, mon Lieutenant."

"Now, the main reason Perviz al Bahman keeps hurling his men against us is Morgiana."

"Oui, mon Lieutenant."

"But Morgiana is not here. She's gone like so much powder smoke in a wind. As long as Perviz al Bahman thinks she is in here, he will continue to attack and attack hard. If he knew she wasn't here, what would he do?"

"Maybe he'd let up."

"Right. As long as she is not here, we have that much less to fight for. For her sake I was willing to hold out. I am not willing now. Hunger and thirst, Sergeant. I propose two things: that we tell Perviz al Bahman she is gone, and that we abandon the post."

"But, *mon Lieutenant*, there are Jeppas in the hills. We have no refuge if we leave the fort. We will be caught up one by one and slaughtered."

"Starvation is not a soldier's death. Sergeant, I do not know what this is all about, this attack."

"Why, it is simple! Perviz al Bahman wants the lady, yes?"

"Not as simple as that. We were put here as decoys and left in the lurch. Somehow, Ibn Batuta and the Jeppas are mixed up in this, and—most likely—Morgiana. It might be cold fact, but I think it is certain that we were placed in a position where the caid would attack us. Perhaps Ibn Batuta, a clever man, realizes that the caid would be wiped out by the next onslaught from the main command which will come to avenge our death. Ibn Batuta, I believe, wanted the scalp of the caid. He furnished provocation for Perviz al Bahman to attack. We die, the Legion comes and the caid dies. Any way I can see it, Sergeant, we stand to lose our good health."

"But *mon Dieu, mon Lieutenant,* if that is so, there is certainly no way out for us."

"Perhaps and perhaps not. I think this is one time when it is possible for the pawn to reach a king row and become an offensive piece. We *will* get out. But we'll have to run against rather high odds. Notice, Sergeant, that the attack comes from the west. The north wall opens to a hillside. There is a postern there. When night comes, I will violate one of the foremost military laws. Under a flag of truce, I shall inform Perviz al Bahman that Morgiana has departed. While I speak to him, you will evacuate the fort."

"And leave you in front? No! I will not do it."

"You must do it. While the caid is thinking over the startling news, I withdraw into the gate. They will doubtless try to charge while the gate is open. I will make certain that they do. Piccard will stand ready with a Hotchkiss. We will pile all our grenades and our mountain gun shells beside the gate. The Hotchkiss fires, I withdraw, Piccard and I run for it leaving the gate open. The men on the north wall will be sucked around to the west by the commotion. The caid will enter the fort and . . . well, there it is."

The sergeant shook his head over the certain death of the Lieutenant, but he knew an order when he heard one. The sergeant's gloom deepened when he observed that the Lieutenant was terribly cheerful again. Too cheerful. The Lieutenant would save the sergeant and the men, but the Lieutenant, in doing so, would die.

But an order is an order and sergeants are sergeants and the Lieutenant was commandant, and through the long hot day the fight went on.

During the lulls, the grenades and ammunition were massed beside the gate, precious water was used to moisten dirt and a giant mudpack was put over the pile, making thereby a bomb of tremendous proportions.

The Lieutenant joked about it. He said that this was a

mighty big pill, but then the caid had a mighty big stomach and was awfully sick. As a physician, the Lieutenant claimed great powers. He said he could cure at least a hundred Harj citizens of anything from toothache to mange in less than five seconds. He said that as a pharmacist he had long studied this formula and had never seen it fail with Berbers and Arabs. He told Jehan that the French Medical Association would award him any number of prizes and certificates, but that he was neither grasping nor vain and would accept only the most useless, such as maybe a couple bottles of cognac.

Every hour or two, the Lieutenant would find something else to add to his pill. Some spikes, a broken keg, and even his own alarm clock, so that "the caid can tell the time and not keep the devil waiting any."

The sergeant grew gloomier and gloomier, seeing the Lieutenant in such a high state of merriment. Germaine knew that the Lieutenant fully expected to die.

At four that blistering afternoon, the Lieutenant touched the arm of small, weasel-faced Legionnaire Schmaltz.

"Special duty," said the Lieutenant, grinning. "Follow me."

They went down to the late quarters of Morgiana which had remained untouched. Schmaltz, all agog, could not believe his ears when he heard himself commanded to dress in the raiment of the girl.

He was not at all certain in his suspicious soul that he was not to become the butt of a joke. However, orders were orders and he snaked off his sweat-stained khaki and, with clumsy, fumbling fingers, dressed himself in the filmy, sheer balloon trousers, girdle, veil and slippers. He put a cloak about his shoulders and then, feeling very embarrassed, confronted his officer.

"Magnificent!" crowed the Lieutenant. "Here, wait."

He took some kohl and darkened Schmaltz's eyes. He adjusted the cloak and the veil until Schmaltz looked, to a casual observer more than a hundred meters distant, like Morgiana.

Red and squirming, Schmaltz was led up the steps to the battlement. Powder-stained, heat-blistered Legionnaires turned, gaped and then guffawed. Schmaltz tried to run, but the Lieutenant had him.

"My arm, fair lady," said the Lieutenant.

Schmaltz obeyed, mystified and annoyed though he might be. For a cutthroat of great talent, this was a strange role.

Firing stopped on the Harj roofs. A lull came in the fighting. Headcloths began to appear above sandbags and over abutments.

"No firing," cautioned the Lieutenant.

Up and down the battlement the two paraded, and every time they passed an embrasure they were in full view of the Arabs and Berbers.

The farce lasted for more than fifteen minutes. Then the Lieutenant led Schmaltz down the steps and allowed him to dress again. But try as he might, Schmaltz could not remove the black stain of the kohl from his eyes.

The Lieutenant sought out the sergeant. "They're sure she is here now. Make it hot and heavy for the next two hours, send down the men in three sections to *empaquetage*. Abandon all useless material and wreck everything you have to leave."

"Lieutenant, I can't let you do this. It is folly. You will get shot and killed, and what good will it do us if you are gone?"

The Lieutenant grinned. "It's all my fault that you're here. To hell with what happens. I've been buried once. I'll be buried again, perhaps. If you disobey me," he added, negligently flicking at his boots with his crop, "you're making yourself responsible for the lives of fifty-seven men. Carry on, Sergeant."

"Oui, mon Lieutenant."

An hour crept by, and then another. The sun went down in a fanfare of gold and blue and red. A rose stain was upon the Atlas, gradually receding toward the peaks.

It was, thought the Lieutenant, a nice evening to die.

He went to his quarters and took a white shirt from his locker. He went to the watchtower, impaled the garment upon a bayonet and handed it to Piccard.

"Mon enfant," said the Lieutenant to the grizzled old veteran, "you and I may be about to fight our last fight. Let's make it hot for those grasshoppers, eh? You train your Hotchkiss on the gate from the opposite wall. Hold this flag against the battlement. I am going out, alone, to talk with Perviz al Bahman. I am going to wheel and dash inside without shutting the gate.

"You are to cut the devil out of them, then I'll blow up that big pill by shooting a clip into the detonators. In the smoke,

61

we may possibly have a chance to get away. But if I am shot before I reach the fort, turn the machine gun on the pill and try to get out yourself. Am I understood?"

"Oui, mon Lieutenant."

"Sergeant! It's dark. Withdraw everyone, mass them at the postern on the north wall. March fast, make no sound and go like hell. You may be able to get through to the main command."

"Oui, mon Lieutenant."

The sergeant stood stiff as a gun barrel. He saluted and there was a suspicion of moisture in his eyes. He about-faced, roared orders in a brass voice. Men came from the embrasures. They were in full pack.

The white flag had been sighted. Firing dropped off by degrees and finally the world was still beneath a cloak of thin twilight.

Piccard sat on his gun tripod, waiting.

The Lieutenant lifted the heavy bars on the gate.

Hobnails grated. The Legionnaires moved out of sight down the long tunnel which led to the low postern on the north wall.

The Lieutenant set his kepi over one eye, spun his riding crop, pulled open the gate. His face was smiling, his eyes bright and laughing.

Carelessly, he walked out into full view. Any Berber or Arab in the houses could have shot him in that instant, but they did not.

Quiet prevailed.

The hoofbeats of a horse came slowly toward the fort.

In the wide street, the Lieutenant met Perviz al Bahman.

The caid was sitting on a big white horse. It took a big horse to hold him. He sagged in the saddle. His brows sagged. His stomach was squashy against the horse's neck.

In a weary voice, the caid said, "You have come to surrender her?"

"That all depends," said the Lieutenant, stalling for darkness. "What terms am I offered?"

"No terms."

"Oh, but we have plenty of food and water."

Perviz al Bahman sighed. "This is foolish of you. You know that I intend to kill you anyway. Why not give up now, Commandant? And then, of course, you could give me Morgiana. I need that woman for political reasons, Commandant. You have no right to interfere."

The talk went on. Bit by bit the glow of the Atlas died and the world became black.

It was time.

Suddenly the Lieutenant cried, "I mean to keep her and hold you back. And you and your troops, you misbegotten pig, can go whistle up *Shaitan* for all that I care."

Viciously he reached out and brought his riding crop across the caid's fat face. The sound of it was like a pistol shot.

Turning, the Lieutenant sprinted for the fort.

Voice screeching with rage, the caid shouted, "Kill! Kill him! Rush the gate!"

Mannlichers, Sniders, Mausers, opened up like rattling snare drums. Rock dust and sand spurted about the Lieutenant's running feet.

*Voice screeching with rage, the caid shouted,
"Kill! Kill him! Rush the gate!"*

With shrill yells, *"Allah-il-Allah,"* the warriors streamed down from the houses, from around the walls of the fort, pouring like swooping vultures toward the fort gate.

A slug twitched the Lieutenant's sleeve. Another grazed his shoulder and he still had thirty feet to go.

Suddenly his leg went numb and doubled under him. He rolled, tried to get up, clawed desperately on his hands and knees to make the yawning portals before him.

The howling pack closed upon him, but he was not yet taken.

Scrambling, dragging his helpless boot behind him, he got inside and ducked into the protection of an inner sentry box.

The Hotchkiss opened.

The gateway was jammed. Men went down as though a tight line stretched across the entrance had tripped them all together. Behind them, impeded by the suddenly dead, the warriors tried to push on.

The Hotchkiss rolled and rattled.

The Lieutenant, sweating, face drawn, eyes like live coals, crawled down the wall, turned at right angles and tried to get at his gun.

A big shadow loomed over him. Great arms scooped him up and carried him. He swore and tried to struggle. It was Jehan, who had stayed behind without orders in case something of this sort happened.

Piccard was hammering away at the abundant targets, but not even the machine gun could stem the tide which rolled in waves through the gate.

Jehan stumbled toward a postern in the south wall. Piccard saw them, stripped the breech from the Hotchkiss and plunged after them.

The Lieutenant tried to make them leave him, but they would not go. With Jehan at his head and Piccard at his feet, he was carried through the low, hidden door and outside the fort.

Howling with rage and screaming for blood, the Harj fighters rushed through the fort, only to find it empty.

Mystified, the captains sought out Perviz al Bahman, who had kept well out of the way of the Hotchkiss.

But Perviz al Bahman had no solution. He did not know that the Legionnaires were heading north at double time, and that the Lieutenant was being carried south, and that Morgiana had been gone from there for days.

Baffled, the caid did the next best thing. He took possession of the fort.

The Lieutenant knew what would happen. His only hope was that the sergeant could get away and make the pass before daylight.

As for himself, Jehan and Piccard, they might be able to hide and . . .

Before the three, a ring of white robes rose out of the dark. Leveled rifles and ready swords silently commanded them to halt.

The Lieutenant squirmed around and looked at them. He was taken after all.

Well, that was that. It was fun while it lasted.

CHAPTER SIX

A Prisoner Gives Orders

THE room was dim, of a dingy brown color, and it smelled strongly of dead goats and sweat.

The light came in, in a single slit which shifted slowly along the floor and then up until it touched the face of the Lieutenant, waking him.

He raised himself up a little and then sank back, wondering where he was and why, and who else might be here. Gradually the memory of the escape came back to him. Jehan and Piccard had been carrying him. Where were they now?

He wondered what the caid, Perviz al Bahman, would do to him. Something drastic, no doubt. Something in keeping with the general good taste of caids, who were a law unto themselves. Something which would have to do with knives or fire or, and better, a nice quick firing squad.

He fell to wondering about Morgiana. He would be able to take it better if he knew she was safe. He was too drowsy to further analyze his thoughts or to wonder just why he should be so concerned about the woman who, it seemed, had aided in setting a trap for him.

His leg ached and he rose up again to see with some astonishment that it was wrapped in linen bandages. His boot lay in the middle of the floor, top fallen over, covered with dust.

The bullet, his fingers told him, had passed through the muscles of his thigh. It was not serious unless infection set in.

He had not been long awake before the door to the room opened, admitting sunlight and a lean, cadaverous-looking man the Lieutenant had not seen before.

This fellow was clean-shaven. His cheeks were sunken in and his eyes were deep cavities in his skull. He was dressed in a woolen djellaba and looked like a hooded monk straight from the chambers of the Inquisition.

"I am Caid Kirzigh, Commandant."

The Lieutenant was so startled he sat erect. "Caid Kirzigh? Then I am in the hands of the Jeppas and not Perviz al Bahman?"

"Correct, Commandant. My men were hanging on the outskirts of the fight and they picked you up."

"But then . . . what about two of my Legionnaires and perhaps a courier?"

"They are here. All three."

The Lieutenant breathed a sigh of relief. That possibly meant that Germaine and all the rest had gotten through to the pass.

"What are you going to do with me?" said the Lieutenant, calmly.

"That I do not know," said the lean caid, squatting on his heels, half his face in brilliant light, the other half deep in the shadow of his cowl. "Your position, Commandant, is a precarious one. You antagonized Perviz al Bahman. Did your superiors order you to do that?"

"No."

"You were unlucky enough to buy Morgiana. Do you know what that means now?"

"Perhaps," said the Lieutenant.

"Finally, you deserted your post. And very foolishly."

"I can't see that it's foolish to try to save your command, my caid."

"But you did not save your command, my brilliant officer. Your sergeant, forty-seven men and eight wounded are all here."

The Lieutenant's heart fell but he showed none of it in his voice or on his face. "If they are all alive, there was no fight."

"No, they did not fight. They surrendered easily."

"I do not believe that, my caid. I know my men."

"You know them when you are leading them. You do not know them without your guidance. There is a difference, Commandant."

"I still do not believe it."

"Never mind, it is true. Commandant, you have been the victim of a trap. Had you held out until the dawn long since past, you would have suffered no defeat."

"I did not know that and nobody considered it important to tell me."

"You might have guessed."

The Lieutenant smiled. "One does not guess when food, water and ammunition get low."

"Ah, well, it does not change matters, Commandant. It remains that you are here, my prisoner. It remains that your men are here. And it seems that there is a slight debt. After all, Commandant, you purchased Morgiana. I cannot forget that."

The Lieutenant heard footsteps outside. Another man entered. A small, limping man in dirty rags. It was Ibn Batuta with his ingratiating smile and his whining voice.

"Good day, *mon Lieutenant*," said Ibn Batuta. "Is your friend the caid gloating over you?"

The Lieutenant was not smiling now. He looked holes into the old man. "He is, Judas."

Ibn Batuta paled and stepped hurriedly back. "No, no! You do not understand—"

"Quiet," said the caid. "Your plans have gone amiss."

"But I was only trying—"

"Quiet!" said the caid. And then to the Lieutenant, "You are here, your men are here. Within the hour I could execute the lot of you and no one would ever know."

"Except, of course, the Legion," said the Lieutenant.

"Not even the Legion. Commandant, the lines across the Atlas are closed. Your main command is busy elsewhere. This post at Harj is outside their combat lines, completely isolated. You are deserted. Now come, will you have bullets or—"

"My caid," said the Lieutenant, "if you think it is necessary for you to make bargains with me, you are wrong. I begin to understand this thing. Morgiana was captured by the men of Harj. Ibn Batuta, controlling the slave market, kept her capture dark until he was able to offer her to me. He gave me the money to buy her. That money went instantly back to him.

"The stage was set for a fight between Perviz al Bahman,

who wanted Morgiana, and myself, who had Morgiana. No doubt about her safety existed in either your mind or Ibn Batuta's. You knew she could take care of herself.

"My blunder, gentlemen, becomes apparent. When I had cut Perviz al Bahman's troops down to size and had exhausted them with a continued siege, while they were bunched about the fort like so many sheep for slaughter, you of Jeppa intended to attack and catch them in a vice and take Harj. Am I right?"

The caid scowled but nodded. Ibn Batuta averted his eyes and denied nothing.

"One of your men," said the Lieutenant, "aided her to climb out of the fort in the night in the guise of a Harj fighter. Morgiana is here, unharmed. Certainly you have made a mess of things by not taking me into your confidence."

"How could we know that you would not turn on us and make peace with Perviz al Bahman in that manner?" said the caid. "You might have kept Morgiana—"

"Enough. When you try to ally yourself with a body of Legionnaires, my caid, it is expedient that you tell them the basis of your strategy. I know now what this is all about because, my caid, you have not asked me about Morgiana. She must be here, which includes you in the scheme."

"I am here," said a small voice outside.

Morgiana, wrapped in a silvery cloak, stepped into the doorway. The Lieutenant smiled at her.

"Ah," he said, "there you are, my pretty little slave."

"Greetings, my lord and master," said Morgiana in a sarcastic voice. "What would Your Excellency have this evening?"

"My kingdom for a horse," said the Lieutenant.

71

"Eh?" said the caid, blankly.

"I said a horse and I meant a horse, my caid. Also, may I have my troops, my sword and pistol and a few hundred of your cavalry."

"You are mad!" cried the caid.

"Pleasantly so," added Morgiana. "Why do you want these things, my fine prisoner?"

"Because I hate parleys. Your caid comes here all solemn and mouthy to threaten me into doing something for him. He did not take Germaine unless he told Germaine that it would be to the Legion's advantage. I do not like threats. I do not like moneylenders. I do not like that thing you think is intrigue. Hence, my horse, my sword, my men. And be quick about it, little serf."

She hesitated, with a glance at the caid.

"Commandant," said the caid, "I cannot quite understand—"

"Bah!" cried the Lieutenant. "What am I to you but a tool? I am a man in a uniform. I have no identity but that of a commanding officer to you. You think you can use me. You want Perviz al Bahman out of the way. I want to regain the command of Harj—"

"But Perviz al Bahman has the fort!" cried Ibn Batuta.

"He won't have it long," snapped the Lieutenant. "Kirzigh, prepare yourself to take the town of Harj. I will take the fort."

"But Perviz al Bahman with three thousand men failed to take it," protested the caid. "I thought if we could combine our forces we might lay siege to Harj and after some weeks—"

"Too slow. I was commanding the fort before. I am attacking the fort now. There is, my caid, my slave and my Judas, a vast difference. Quick! Do not stand there. Beat drums, blow bugles, roar commands! Come, my slave, do we ride together on the same path tonight or do we differ again?"

Morgiana had nothing to say. She backed against the wall and watched the three men go outside.

The Lieutenant took a long mountain rifle roughly from the hands of a sentry. He inverted it, tucked the butt under his arm and used it as a crutch.

Before him on the hillside he saw his Legionnaires. They were camped in regulation style, were in complete possession of themselves and their weapons.

Jean Patou, the runner, came quickly to his officer. "They stopped me before I could get through, sir."

"I know. Sergeant! Light marching order. Issue all ammunition. Bugler, assembly. Piccard, attend the machine guns. Jehan, get me a bag of grenades, like a good lad."

Bugle blended with the slap and clank of equipment, voices hoarse and hurried, the Legion camp came to pieces in less time than the Lieutenant could turn and mount the horse which had been brought up for him.

The mount was a big Arabian, all white, and the saddle was silver. To the pommel he strapped his bag of grenades and sat waiting for his men to fall into line. The Lieutenant's leg was dully aching but he did not notice it. His eyes were alight and he sat straighter than a bayonet in the saddle.

Some distance away, the Jeppas were mounting and falling into rank under the stentorian commands of the caid himself. Morgiana was not in sight and the Lieutenant experienced a feeling of regret.

The caid, on a cream-colored stallion, approached and saluted.

"I am to attack the fort and take it," said the Lieutenant. "You will attack the town itself. Most of its defenses—such as Perviz al Bahman's house—are reduced by shellfire from my mountain gun. You should have no difficulty, as many of the Harj men are probably combing these hills for my men, myself and Morgiana. How far is it to Harj?"

"About six kilometers, Commandant. Allow me to say that I am afraid your plan—"

"Will not work?" said the Lieutenant.

"Well . . . it seems foolhardy. If three thousand men could not capture sixty in the fort, how can the reversed position succeed, eh?"

"Wait and see, my caid."

"Commandant, if you do this thing, you can ask and receive anything of me up to and including my harem. But I doubt—"

"Fall in! Squaaaads, right! Columnnnn, left! March!"

With a salute to the caid, the Lieutenant led off toward Harj.

"Route march!"

The column swung down a defile in the mountains toward the town. The Legionnaires were silent lest they draw down a Harj patrol upon themselves and so announce their coming prematurely. The only sounds were slapping rifle slings, creaking leather and steady footfalls.

The night fell before they had gone far. After that, they stumbled down a rough and twisting trail, barely able to see the Lieutenant's horse before them.

Germaine grumbled from time to time but he felt very good.

The Lieutenant was so certain of himself that all doubts were laid aside and forgotten.

That it was quite possible an ambush lay between them and Harj did not worry the Lieutenant. He had two automatic riflemen, one on either side of him. He and the white horse would get the first shock of the fire from any patrol.

He was not worrying about his awkward position at all. That he had deserted his post in the face of enemy fire was quite justifiable, even sensible. That he was about to attack the same post against overwhelming odds was all that interested him at the moment.

Three kilometers, four kilometers, five kilometers, and they could see the lights of the town.

CHAPTER SEVEN

Thunder Over the Fort

PERVIZ AL BAHMAN hardly expected an attack from so small a force, but for fear of what might come from the Jeppa, he had the place well fortified, the fort garrisoned, arms and ammunition in readiness, sentries posted everywhere.

The caid was proceeding circuitously to come upon the town from the west.

Perviz al Bahman was about to get a surprise there in the Lieutenant's quarters.

"Silence, *mes enfants*," said the Lieutenant. "We wait here for a few moments."

Almost in the shadow of the fort, the Legionnaires leaned upon their rifles and rested.

Voices could be heard in the town. The moon was up, and along the fort walls sentries could be seen, djellabas billowing in the faint breeze as they walked past the embrasures.

Half an hour passed and then, like a clap of thunder, the caid struck the town from the other side.

Rifles and yells blended in a staccato blare. The town's outposts were being ridden down and rolled back into the streets.

"It is time," said the Lieutenant. "They have closed the fort gates." Rapidly he called off the names of twenty of the outfit's best marksmen. "Take your posts on the roofs across from the fort. There are twenty embrasures. One man to an opening. Fire into those slits as fast as you can. Let no warrior put his neck out. Germaine, with the remaining men, station yourself up the street from the gate."

"And you, *mon Lieutenant*?" said Germaine.

"I will attack the fort."

"You?" chorused the men, aghast. "Alone?"

"*Mon Lieutenant*," said Germaine. "You are wounded. You cannot—"

"I'll never get off my horse. At my signal, Sergeant, charge. You riflemen on the roofs, wheel and face the approach streets. Hotchkiss gunners will cover any access to the fort from the outside. If the devils attack after we have attacked the fort, keep them back."

"My God," said Germaine, "you are mad, *mon Lieutenant*. What can you do?"

"Follow my orders and wear medals. Forget them and wear shrouds. *En avant!*"

Quickly, their noise hidden by the uproar on the other side of Harj, the Legionnaires moved into position. The roofs were deserted as the Lieutenant knew they would be. But the sandbags were still there.

The gates were closed to the fort. Sentries, sighting the moving shadows against the sky, shouted the alarm.

Twenty Lebels went into action, rapid fire.

No embrasure on that wall could be used. Steel-jacketed slugs were combing them, closing them, making them suicide posts.

The Lieutenant posted the sergeant and his men. And

then, riding at a trot as though on parade, easily seen in the golden moonlight, the Lieutenant went straight down the street to the gate in plain sight.

A Berber tried to shoot through an embrasure. A Lebel got him. Another tried to crack down from the watchtower. A Hotchkiss tore him to pieces as he plummeted earthward.

The Lieutenant came under the shadow of the walls. From his saddle he lifted his sack and extracted a grenade. Then, with an over swinging motion, he threw the bomb far, far up against the moon, over the parapet and out of sight.

A small explosion followed.

"Missed," said the Lieutenant, quieting his mount.

With his teeth he pulled a second pin. Carefully, throwing more to the right, he sent that grenade soaring. It vanished.

The Lieutenant wheeled his Arabian and dashed clear of the gate.

With a concussion which made the ears ache and the eyes pop, a terrible detonation sounded just inside the wall. The pill the Lieutenant had been unable to use before, looking so innocent under its mud pie, had been ignited by the grenade.

Rocks, locks, splinters and men went skyward. The whole wall blew out and left a gaping hole where the gate had been.

The Lieutenant, before the dust and debris could even start down, bawled, "Charge!"

Germaine and his men came down the street at a run, bayonets glittering, faces set for slaughter.

The riflemen on the roofs turned and caught another attacking force from the other side of Harj upon the point of their quick bullets.

The Lieutenant reined his horse through and into the smoke. On his heels came his Legionnaires.

With screams of terror the remaining Berbers and Arabs tried vainly to protect themselves.

In a matter of seconds, bayonets flashed, arms were thrown down and the valiant warriors were standing with hands grabbing at the moon.

The Lieutenant rode his horse straight up the steps to his quarters. Perviz al Bahman rushed out in an attempt to get away. The Lieutenant had him by a roll of loose flesh.

Dragging the ex-caid with him, the Lieutenant rode on down to the compound where the dust and smoke of the explosion still lingered.

For a few minutes, Lebels and Hotchkiss roared outside and then they too were silent.

Caught between Caid Kirzigh and the bristling roofs, the remainder of Perviz al Bahman's forces surrendered to a man and begged for mercy.

Perviz al Bahman was whining and moaning.

Caid Kirzigh and some of his captains rode through the gate and came to a halt before the Lieutenant.

"By Allah!" cried Kirzigh. "I know not how you did it, I know only that you are a *soldier*!"

"My caid," said the Lieutenant to Kirzigh, "much as I would like to let you have this tub of lard here for execution, I feel that it would be more prudent for me to send him to Fez where he will be imprisoned for an armed attack against France. I think also that you should appoint some loyal captain as magistrate for Harj. There will be no caid . . ."

"But Commandant!" cried Kirzigh. "I have only undertaken—"

"You will get none of these spoils, my caid. Neither you nor your friend Ibn Batuta. I will give you enough leeway so that this feud between Jeppa and Harj will cease. Other than that, you can have nothing. I am Commandant here. You yourself are caught between machine guns on those roofs outside and my Legionnaires on these battlements. I have not been fighting a war for you, but for France. There my allegiance lies. I am sorry that I cannot account you victor. I thank you for your help, but any future outbreak either here or in Jeppa will result in your instant arrest. Am I understood?"

Caid Kirzigh had not reckoned with his man. He was trapped by his own intrigue.

For a moment it looked like fight. There in the bright moonlight, the Lieutenant and the caid stared hostilely at each other.

The caid was the first to drop his eyes. The Lieutenant relaxed and smiled.

"Now that that is settled, my caid, now that there will be lasting peace in these hills no matter the position of the main command, now that you know what the Legion can do when it wishes, I claim that favor even unto your harem."

"No!" cried Kirzigh.

"You gave it, I claim it, or at least in part."

"What do you mean?" said the caid.

A rider moved slowly out of the group. Morgiana came to the Lieutenant's side and sat there quietly looking at him. Pride, respect and love were in her calm eyes.

"I claim the right to marry Morgiana," said the Lieutenant. "If she will have me."

"I cannot," said the caid, "allow a woman of the Jeppa to marry an outsider. It is impossible. And no matter your machine guns, Commandant, I still have my sword at my side. And no matter what Morgiana thinks, I mean what I say. No woman of the Jeppa will ever marry a *Franzawi*."

Ibn Batuta, mounted upon a mule, came to the front. He looked at the caid and was amused.

"You thought this idea good in the first place," said Ibn Batuta. "While you have not achieved command of Harj, I have achieved the safety I wanted from Perviz al Bahman. I stand ready to help *mon Lieutenant*."

"Traitor," snapped Kirzigh, angrily.

"If I am a traitor, then you, by inference, are a liar." Ibn Batuta was very humorous about it.

"A liar!" shrieked the caid.

"*Ai*," said Ibn Batuta. "A liar. Your women of Jeppa are not good. How do you think such a jewel as Morgiana ever came to you as a daughter?"

"You . . . you brought her to me as a child," said the caid, simmering down a little.

"Yes. As a child. I have here certain documents I meant someday to give her. She came to you, my caid, as a daughter because I commanded it. She was taken, if you remember, from the American Legation at Casablanca at the original sacking of that town seventeen years ago. Her father, the man in charge, and her mother were both killed. I bought her from the raiders and brought her here. *I* paid the expenses of her education in Fez. *I* have made certain of her treatment because of the hold I have over you, Kirzigh. Am I right?"

The caid looked hard at Ibn Batuta and then dropped his eyes and nodded.

"And if anyone is to give this girl away, it is I." Ibn Batuta laughed about it. "I suspected that this would happen. I knew it when I saw the Lieutenant and knew him to be an American. Race calls to race and she has never cared for the youths of the mountains. Come, Commandant, she is yours and a goodly dowry goes with her."

Morgiana was too astonished to do or say anything. She looked oddly at the Lieutenant and then her gaze softened and she began to smile.

The Lieutenant smiled back.

"As Allah wills, my lord and master."

She gave him her hand and he kissed it, looking up into her warm eyes.

"He wills well, my pretty slave," said the Lieutenant.

"It's good politics anyway," muttered the cynical Germaine into his tangled brown beard.

High above them in the moonlight were the Atlas, ghostly and still, at peace.

Story Preview

Story Preview

NOW that you've just ventured through one of the captivating tales in the Stories from the Golden Age collection by L. Ron Hubbard, turn the page and enjoy a preview of *The Black Sultan*. Join fugitive Eddie Moran, who's on the run from the French Foreign Legion. When he saves the life of a deposed Berber ruler, Eddie finds himself in the middle of a war, captured by the Black Sultan, usurper of the Berber's throne.

The Black Sultan

*A**MERICAIN!*" bawled *Capitaine* Nicolle. "Put up—"
As swift as striking snakes, hands darted for gun boots.
A scimitar flashed like silver lightning and the barbs lunged
forward—straight toward Godfrey Harrison!

I thought for an instant that I would see a dead vice-consul.
It was inevitable. It had happened too fast. And I was as
surprised as the others when the .45 Colt came away from
my ribs and started to jar my palm.

A scimitar was coming down. As well as I could, I spotted
the base of the djellaba hood and fired. The man reared up
straight. The sword clanged against the pavement and the
Berber came tumbling out of his saddle limply.

The other Berber whirled about, trying to level his Snider.
He caught a bullet in his teeth and I saw the sick roll of his
eyes as he began to slide down.

I was aware, standing wreathed in my own powder smoke,
that the girl was staring at me, not at the dead men. Camel
boys tugged at their halters and the caravan plunged down
the curving street.

A hawk-faced rider paused, saw me raise the gun, and
thought better of valor. He was lost in the welter of dust
which rose from escaping hoofs.

The two French officers were still there, pressed back against a wall like life-size toy soldiers. I suppose they thought they were next.

Godfrey Harrison swabbed at the sweatband of his pith helmet and tottered across to me.

"My God, Eddie," he quavered, "that was close! But why, oh why did you do it? You're in hot water now—bad enough without all that."

Behind Harrison came the silk-robed gentleman, face impassive. His fingers rested lightly on the tip of his blond beard and I thought I saw a twinkle in his blue eyes.

Deciding they were not to be targets, the two Frenchmen bristled and strode up. *Capitaine* Nicolle was snorting like a winded horse.

"Ah, so that is it!" cried Nicolle. "You destroy the peace of Morocco. You carry dangerous weapons. You attack our citizens without provocation. Now, *Americain*, we will send you back."

"Back where?" I demanded.

He pried my fingers off my gun and took it from me. "Back to French Indochina! We know you, so do not pretend. You are that so infamous Edward Moran, enemy of France. Ah, but we have orders concerning you!"

The big tribesman stepped easily forward. "Allow me," he said in French, "to introduce myself."

With an insolence only a Frenchman can achieve, they turned their backs upon him and fastened upon my arms.

I planted my boot heels and balked. Godfrey Harrison swabbed anew at his sweatband and sputtered.

"I say," mourned Godfrey. "You can't do that, you know. He's an American citizen and—"

I wonder why it is most of our consuls in faraway spots must affect a British accent.

They paid no attention whatever to Harrison, and his eyes were sad and watery behind the spectacles perched on his thin nose. The officers were putting their backs to the task. My heels were skidding, raising small whirlpools of dust. Berbers stopped and watched, crowding to obtain grandstand seats.

The Legion officers were rumpled. They loosed their holds and stepped back straightening their tunics, realizing, doubtless, that a street fight lay far beneath their dignity. After a moment's deliberation Nicolle drew his stumpy revolver and centered the muzzle on my chest.

"Now march!" he commanded. "We do not have to fuss with you, Moran."

"Nor I with you," I replied, dusting my hands and looking at the gun. I hate to be pawed and my temper was rising. "You haven't any order for my arrest."

"Ho!" cried the little one, gazing all about him in mock surprise. "He thinks we need an order for his arrest. He thinks such a victim of Madame Guillotine needs warrants and process of law. He thinks—"

"Hah," echoed the other, "he is crazy. All *Americains* are crazy. He organizes a revolt against France and then escapes, and now—"

"I didn't organize a revolt!" I protested. "I convoyed three Annamite chiefs up the Magat in a speedboat." Which was true. I had also helped them drill their little yellow soldiers, but I hoped France would not know that.

"You came," said the tallest, "on a Trans-African Airliner. You go back by narrow gauge railroad, third class. By that, and in the hold of a smelly tramp. If you manage to arrive alive, you will be executed, but perhaps we should save France that expense."

The big blond stepped up again. He laid firm hands on the epaulets of the two and gently lifted them apart.

"Pardon my intrusion, gentlemen, but my name is El Zidan." He said it so quietly you knew that it meant a great deal.

The Frenchmen gaped. The little one made a noise like a throttled crow.

"El Zidan? But El Zidan is—is—You cannot come like this, openly, to town—"

"I am here," said El Zidan. "That caravan was the property of Abu 'l Hasan, the Black Sultan." He motioned with a disdainful finger at the two lumps of cloth and blood which lay upon the pavement, attracting flies.

"Those men," continued El Zidan, "saw me and knew me. They tried to kill me by riding me down. This Eddie Moran saw it in time, and acted quickly, saving my life. Therefore I intercede for him, and should you gentlemen see fit to make an issue of it, I'm afraid that no more horses will be sent to *la belle Légion*. You are the judge."

The Frenchmen looked too stunned to move, but they managed to salute. Their scarlet pants walked away from there in a military straight line.

Nicolle went about thirty feet and then came back. He shook a finger under my nose and strained his words through his teeth.

"All right, *mon ami*. All right! You have a champion this time. But we have an additional charge against you for killing two men, and carrying concealed weapons. *Monsieur* Moran, I give you twenty-four hours to get out of the town! After that, a Legion patrol will pick you up and throw you in jail awaiting extradition." He glanced at El Zidan. "Horses or no horses!"

To find out more about *The Black Sultan* and how you can obtain your copy, go to www.goldenagestories.com.

Glossary

Glossary

STORIES FROM THE GOLDEN AGE *reflect the words and expressions used in the 1930s and 1940s, adding unique flavor and authenticity to the tales. While a character's speech may often reflect regional origins, it also can convey attitudes common in the day. So that readers can better grasp such cultural and historical terms, uncommon words or expressions of the era, the following glossary has been provided.*

allez-vous-en: (French) be off with you.

Annamite: of Annam, a historic region of southeast Asia, comprising most of central Vietnam. The name Annam, meaning "pacified south," comes from an ancient Chinese name for Vietnam. France revived the term in the nineteenth century to designate central Vietnam. In the 1880s France established a protectorate over the region. Annam, along with Cochin China in southern Vietnam, Tonkin in northern Vietnam and eventually Laos and Cambodia, was part of the French-ruled Indochinese Union, popularly called French Indochina. During World War II, Japan expelled France from occupying Vietnam.

Atlas: Atlas Mountains; a mountain range in northwest Africa extending about fifteen hundred miles through Morocco,

Algeria and Tunisia, including the Rock of Gibraltar. The Atlas range separates the Mediterranean and Atlantic coastlines from the Sahara Desert.

attendre, mon enfant: (French) pay attention, my child.

bandolier: a broad belt worn over the shoulder by soldiers and having a number of small loops or pockets for holding cartridges.

barb: a breed of horses introduced by the Moors (Muslim people of mixed Berber and Arab descent) that resemble Arabian horses and are known for their speed and endurance.

Berber: a member of a people living in North Africa, primarily Muslim, living in settled or nomadic tribes between the Sahara and Mediterranean Sea and between Egypt and the Atlantic Ocean.

billet: to provide lodging for; quarter.

caid: a Berber chieftain.

cap and bells: a cap with bells on it, once worn by jesters. Made of cloth, the cap was floppy with three points, each of which had a jingle bell at the end. The three points of the cap represent the ears and tail of an ass.

caporal: (French) corporal.

Casablanca: a seaport on the Atlantic coast of Morocco.

demoiselle: (French) young lady.

devil-may-care: wildly reckless.

djellaba: a long loose hooded garment with full sleeves, worn especially in Muslim countries.

empaquetage: (French) packing.

en avant: (French) forward.

Fez: the former capital of several dynasties and one of the holiest places in Morocco; it has kept its religious primacy through the ages.

Franzawi: (Arabic) Frenchman.

G-men: government men; agents of the Federal Bureau of Investigation.

hobnail: a short nail with a thick head used to increase the durability of a boot sole.

Hotchkiss: a heavy machine gun designed and manufactured by the Hotchkiss Company in France from the late 1920s until World War II where it saw service with various nations' forces, including France and Japan, where the gun was built under license. The machine gun is named for Benjamin B. Hotchkiss (1826–1885), one of the leading American weapons engineers of his day, who established the company in 1867.

houris: in Muslim belief, any of the dark-eyed virgins of perfect beauty believed to live with the blessed in Paradise.

jinnī: (Arabic) in Muslim legend, a spirit often capable of assuming human or animal form and exercising supernatural influence over people.

kepi: a cap with a circular top and a nearly horizontal visor; a French military cap that men in the Foreign Legion wear.

kohl: a cosmetic preparation used especially in the Middle East to darken the rims of the eyelids.

Lebels: French rifles that were adopted as standard infantry weapons in 1887 and remained in official service until after World War II.

legation: the official headquarters of a diplomatic minister.

Legion: French Foreign Legion, a specialized military unit of the French Army, consisting of volunteers of all nationalities assigned to military operations and duties outside France.

Legionnaires: members of the French Foreign Legion, a unique elite unit within the French Army established in 1831. It was created as a unit for foreign volunteers and was primarily used to protect and expand the French colonial empire during the nineteenth century, but has also taken part in all of France's wars with other European powers. It is known to be an elite military unit whose training focuses not only on traditional military skills, but also on the building of a strong esprit de corps amongst members. As its men come from different countries with different cultures, this is a widely accepted solution to strengthen them enough to work as a team. Training is often not only physically hard with brutal training methods, but also extremely stressful with high rates of desertion.

Magat: a river on the largest island of the Philippines.

Mannlicher: a type of rifle equipped with a manually operated sliding bolt for loading cartridges for firing, as opposed to the more common rotating bolt of other rifles. Mannlicher rifles were considered reasonably strong and accurate.

Maroc: (French) Morocco.

Mauser: a bolt-action rifle made by Mauser, a German arms manufacturer. These rifles have been made since the 1870s.

mes enfants: (French) my children.

metal: mettle; spirited determination.

mon ami: (French) my friend.

mon commandant: (French) my commander.

mon Dieu: (French) my God.

mon Lieutenant: (French) my Lieutenant.

Monsieur: (French) Mr.

mountain gun: an artillery piece designed for use during mountain combat. It is generally capable of being broken down into smaller loads for transport by horse, human, mule or truck. Due to its ability to be broken down into smaller "packages," it is sometimes referred to as a pack gun.

mountain rifle: a very long, ruggedly built rifle designed for use in mountainous terrain.

pig's bladder: a pig's bladder blown up like a balloon and hung on the end of a stick. It was part of a jester's costume and was used as a scepter, a mock symbol of office.

pith helmet: a lightweight hat made from dried pith, the soft spongelike tissue in the stems of most flowering plants. Pith helmets are worn in tropical countries for protection from the sun.

postern: postern gate; small secondary entrance, sometimes concealed, and usually at the rear of a castle or fortress, used as a means to come and go without being seen or as a route of escape.

raiment: clothing; attire.

Rif: Er Rif; a hilly region along the coast of northern Morocco.

Riff: a member of any of several Berber peoples inhabiting the Er Rif. The Berber people of the area remained fiercely independent until they were subdued by French and Spanish forces (1925–1926).

Scheherazade: the female narrator of *The Arabian Nights*, who during one thousand and one adventurous nights saved her life by entertaining her husband, the king, with stories.

scimitar: a curved, single-edged sword of Oriental origin.

sentry go: guard duty; the duty of serving as a sentry.

Shaitan: (Arabic) Satan.

Shilha: the Berber dialect spoken in the mountains of southern Morocco.

shroud: cloth used to wrap bodies for burial.

Snider: a rifle formerly used in the British service. It was invented by American Jacob Snider in the mid-1800s. The Snider was a breech-loading rifle, derived from its muzzle-loading predecessor called the Enfield.

Spahis: light cavalry regiments of the French Army recruited primarily from Algeria, Tunisia and Morocco.

Toledo: Toledo, Spain; a city renowned for making swords of finely tempered steel.

tramp: a freight vessel that does not run regularly between fixed ports, but takes a cargo wherever shippers desire.

Tuaregs: members of the nomadic Berber-speaking people of the southwestern Sahara in Africa. They have traditionally engaged in herding, agriculture and convoying caravans across their territories. The Tuaregs became among the most hostile of all the colonized peoples of French West

Africa, because they were among the most affected by colonial policies. In 1917, they fought a vicious and bloody war against the French, but they were defeated and as a result, dispossessed of traditional grazing lands. They are known to be fierce warriors; European explorers expressed their fear by warning, "The scorpion and the Tuareg are the only enemies you meet in the desert."

under the hammer: for sale at public auction.

vizier: a high officer in a Muslim government.

volley fire: simultaneous artillery fire in which each piece is fired a specified number of rounds without regard to the other pieces, and as fast as accuracy will permit.

L. Ron Hubbard
in the Golden Age
of Pulp Fiction

*In writing an adventure story
a writer has to know that he is adventuring
for a lot of people who cannot.
The writer has to take them here and there
about the globe and show them
excitement and love and realism.
As long as that writer is living the part of an
adventurer when he is hammering
the keys, he is succeeding with his story.*

*Adventuring is a state of mind.
If you adventure through life, you have a
good chance to be a success on paper.*

*Adventure doesn't mean globe-trotting,
exactly, and it doesn't mean great deeds.
Adventuring is like art.
You have to live it to make it real.*

—*L. RON HUBBARD*

L. Ron Hubbard
and American
Pulp Fiction

BORN March 13, 1911, L. Ron Hubbard lived a life at least as expansive as the stories with which he enthralled a hundred million readers through a fifty-year career.

Originally hailing from Tilden, Nebraska, he spent his formative years in a classically rugged Montana, replete with the cowpunchers, lawmen and desperadoes who would later people his Wild West adventures. And lest anyone imagine those adventures were drawn from vicarious experience, he was not only breaking broncs at a tender age, he was also among the few whites ever admitted into Blackfoot society as a bona fide blood brother. While if only to round out an otherwise rough and tumble youth, his mother was that rarity of her time—a thoroughly educated woman—who introduced her son to the classics of Occidental literature even before his seventh birthday.

But as any dedicated L. Ron Hubbard reader will attest, his world extended far beyond Montana. In point of fact, and as the son of a United States naval officer, by the age of eighteen he had traveled over a quarter of a million miles. Included therein were three Pacific crossings to a then still mysterious Asia, where he ran with the likes of Her British Majesty's agent-in-place

for North China, and the last in the line of Royal Magicians from the court of Kublai Khan. For the record, L. Ron Hubbard was also among the first Westerners to gain admittance to forbidden Tibetan monasteries below Manchuria, and his photographs of China's Great Wall long graced American geography texts.

L. Ron Hubbard, left, at Congressional Airport, Washington, DC, 1931, with members of George Washington University flying club.

Upon his return to the United States and a hasty completion of his interrupted high school education, the young Ron Hubbard entered George Washington University. There, as fans of his aerial adventures may have heard, he earned his wings as a pioneering barnstormer at the dawn of American aviation. He also earned a place in free-flight record books for the longest sustained flight above Chicago. Moreover, as a roving reporter for *Sportsman Pilot* (featuring his first professionally penned articles), he further helped inspire a generation of pilots who would take America to world airpower.

Immediately beyond his sophomore year, Ron embarked on the first of his famed ethnological expeditions, initially to then untrammeled Caribbean shores (descriptions of which would later fill a whole series of West Indies mystery-thrillers). That the Puerto Rican interior would also figure into the future of Ron Hubbard stories was likewise no accident. For in addition to cultural studies of the island, a 1932–33

LRH expedition is rightly remembered as conducting the first complete mineralogical survey of a Puerto Rico under United States jurisdiction.

There was many another adventure along this vein: As a lifetime member of the famed Explorers Club, L. Ron Hubbard charted North Pacific waters with the first shipboard radio direction finder, and so pioneered a long-range navigation system universally employed until the late twentieth century. While not to put too fine an edge on it, he also held a rare Master Mariner's license to pilot any vessel, of any tonnage in any ocean.

Yet lest we stray too far afield, there is an LRH note at this juncture in his saga, and it reads in part:

"I started out writing for the pulps, writing the best I knew, writing for every mag on the stands, slanting as well as I could."

To which one might add: His earliest submissions date from the summer of 1934, and included tales drawn from true-to-life Asian adventures, with characters roughly modeled on British/American intelligence operatives he had known in Shanghai. His early Westerns were similarly peppered with details drawn from personal

Capt. L. Ron Hubbard in Ketchikan, Alaska, 1940, on his Alaskan Radio Experimental Expedition, the first of three voyages conducted under the Explorers Club flag.

experience. Although therein lay a first hard lesson from the often cruel world of the pulps. His first Westerns were soundly rejected as lacking the authenticity of a Max Brand yarn (a particularly frustrating comment given L. Ron Hubbard's Westerns came straight from his Montana homeland, while Max Brand was a mediocre New York poet named Frederick Schiller Faust, who turned out implausible six-shooter tales from the terrace of an Italian villa).

Nevertheless, and needless to say, L. Ron Hubbard persevered and soon earned a reputation as among the most publishable names in pulp fiction, with a ninety percent placement rate of first-draft manuscripts. He was also among the most prolific, averaging between seventy and a hundred thousand words a month. Hence the rumors that L. Ron Hubbard had redesigned a typewriter for faster keyboard action and pounded out manuscripts on a continuous roll of butcher paper to save the precious seconds it took to insert a single sheet of paper into manual typewriters of the day.

That all L. Ron Hubbard stories did not run beneath said byline is yet another aspect of pulp fiction lore. That is, as publishers periodically rejected manuscripts from top-drawer authors if only to avoid paying top dollar, L. Ron Hubbard and company just as frequently replied with submissions under various pseudonyms. In Ron's case, the list

---

A MAN OF MANY NAMES

Between 1934 and 1950, L. Ron Hubbard authored more than fifteen million words of fiction in more than two hundred classic publications. To supply his fans and editors with stories across an array of genres and pulp titles, he adopted fifteen pseudonyms in addition to his already renowned L. Ron Hubbard byline.

Winchester Remington Colt
Lt. Jonathan Daly
Capt. Charles Gordon
Capt. L. Ron Hubbard
Bernard Hubbel
Michael Keith
Rene Lafayette
Legionnaire 148
Legionnaire 14830
Ken Martin
Scott Morgan
Lt. Scott Morgan
Kurt von Rachen
Barry Randolph
Capt. Humbert Reynolds

included: Rene Lafayette, Captain Charles Gordon, Lt. Scott Morgan and the notorious Kurt von Rachen—supposedly on the lam for a murder rap, while hammering out two-fisted prose in Argentina. The point: While L. Ron Hubbard as Ken Martin spun stories of Southeast Asian intrigue, LRH as Barry Randolph authored tales of

L. Ron Hubbard, circa 1930, at the outset of a literary career that would finally span half a century.

romance on the Western range—which, stretching between a dozen genres is how he came to stand among the two hundred elite authors providing close to a million tales through the glory days of American Pulp Fiction.

In evidence of exactly that, by 1936 L. Ron Hubbard was literally leading pulp fiction's elite as president of New York's American Fiction Guild. Members included a veritable pulp hall of fame: Lester "Doc Savage" Dent, Walter "The Shadow" Gibson, and the legendary Dashiell Hammett—to cite but a few.

Also in evidence of just where L. Ron Hubbard stood within his first two years on the American pulp circuit: By the spring of 1937, he was ensconced in Hollywood, adopting a Caribbean thriller for Columbia Pictures, remembered today as *The Secret of Treasure Island.* Comprising fifteen thirty-minute episodes, the L. Ron Hubbard screenplay led to the most profitable matinée serial in Hollywood history. In accord with Hollywood culture, he was thereafter continually called

111

The 1937 Secret of Treasure Island, *a fifteen-episode serial adapted for the screen by L. Ron Hubbard from his novel,* Murder at Pirate Castle.

upon to rewrite/doctor scripts—most famously for long-time friend and fellow adventurer Clark Gable.

In the interim—and herein lies another distinctive chapter of the L. Ron Hubbard story—he continually worked to open Pulp Kingdom gates to up-and-coming authors. Or, for that matter, anyone who wished to write. It was a fairly unconventional stance, as markets were already thin and competition razor sharp. But the fact remains, it was an L. Ron Hubbard hallmark that he vehemently lobbied on behalf of young authors—regularly supplying instructional articles to trade journals, guest-lecturing to short story classes at George Washington University and Harvard, and even founding his own creative writing competition. It was established in 1940, dubbed the Golden Pen, and guaranteed winners both New York representation and publication in *Argosy*.

But it was John W. Campbell Jr.'s *Astounding Science Fiction* that finally proved the most memorable LRH vehicle. While every fan of L. Ron Hubbard's galactic epics undoubtedly knows the story, it nonetheless bears repeating: By late 1938, the pulp publishing magnate of Street & Smith was determined to revamp *Astounding Science Fiction* for broader readership. In particular, senior editorial director F. Orlin Tremaine called for stories with a stronger *human element*. When acting editor John W. Campbell balked, preferring his spaceship-driven tales,

112

Tremaine enlisted Hubbard. Hubbard, in turn, replied with the genre's first truly *character-driven* works, wherein heroes are pitted not against bug-eyed monsters but the mystery and majesty of deep space itself—and thus was launched the Golden Age of Science Fiction.

The names alone are enough to quicken the pulse of any science fiction aficionado, including LRH friend and protégé, Robert Heinlein, Isaac Asimov, A. E. van Vogt and Ray Bradbury. Moreover, when coupled with LRH stories of fantasy, we further come to what's rightly been described as the foundation of every modern tale of horror: L. Ron Hubbard's immortal *Fear.* It was rightly proclaimed by Stephen King as one of the very few works to genuinely warrant that overworked term "classic"—as in: *"This is a classic tale of creeping, surreal menace and horror. . . . This is one of the really, really good ones."*

L. Ron Hubbard, 1948, among fellow science fiction luminaries at the World Science Fiction Convention in Toronto.

To accommodate the greater body of L. Ron Hubbard fantasies, Street & Smith inaugurated *Unknown*—a classic pulp if there ever was one, and wherein readers were soon thrilling to the likes of *Typewriter in the Sky* and *Slaves of Sleep* of which Frederik Pohl would declare: *"There are bits and pieces from Ron's work that became part of the language in ways that very few other writers managed."*

And, indeed, at J. W. Campbell Jr.'s insistence, Ron was regularly drawing on themes from the Arabian Nights and so introducing readers to a world of genies, jinn, Aladdin and Sinbad—all of which, of course, continue to float through cultural mythology to this day.

At least as influential in terms of post-apocalypse stories was L. Ron Hubbard's 1940 *Final Blackout.* Generally acclaimed as the finest anti-war novel of the decade and among the ten best works of the genre ever authored—here, too, was a tale that would live on in ways few other writers imagined. Hence, the later Robert Heinlein verdict: "Final Blackout *is as perfect a piece of science fiction as has ever been written.*"

Like many another who both lived and wrote American pulp adventure, the war proved a tragic end to Ron's sojourn in the pulps. He served with distinction in four theaters and was highly decorated for commanding corvettes in the North Pacific. He was also grievously wounded in combat, lost many a close friend and colleague and thus resolved to say farewell to pulp fiction and devote himself to what it had supported these many years—namely, his serious research.

Portland, Oregon, 1943; L. Ron Hubbard captain of the US Navy subchaser PC 815.

But in no way was the LRH literary saga at an end, for as he wrote some thirty years later, in 1980:

"Recently there came a period when I had little to do. This was novel in a life so crammed with busy years, and I decided to amuse myself by writing a novel that was pure science fiction."

That work was *Battlefield Earth: A Saga of the Year 3000.* It was an immediate *New York Times* bestseller and, in fact, the first international science fiction blockbuster in decades. It was not, however, L. Ron Hubbard's magnum opus, as that distinction is generally reserved for his next and final work: The 1.2 million word *Mission Earth.*

> **Final Blackout**
> *is as perfect a piece of science fiction as has ever been written.*
>
> —Robert Heinlein

How he managed those 1.2 million words in just over twelve months is yet another piece of the L. Ron Hubbard legend. But the fact remains, he did indeed author a ten-volume *dekalogy* that lives in publishing history for the fact that each and every volume of the series was also a *New York Times* bestseller.

Moreover, as subsequent generations discovered L. Ron Hubbard through republished works and novelizations of his screenplays, the mere fact of his name on a cover signaled an international bestseller. . . . Until, to date, sales of his works exceed hundreds of millions, and he otherwise remains among the most enduring and widely read authors in literary history. Although as a final word on the tales of L. Ron Hubbard, perhaps it's enough to simply reiterate what editors told readers in the glory days of American Pulp Fiction:

He writes the way he does, brothers, because he's been there, seen it and done it!

THE STORIES FROM THE GOLDEN AGE

Your ticket to adventure starts here with the Stories from
the Golden Age collection by master storyteller L. Ron Hubbard.
These gripping tales are set in a kaleidoscope of exotic locales and brim
with fascinating characters, including some of the
most vile villains, dangerous dames and brazen heroes
you'll ever get to meet.

The entire collection of over one hundred and fifty stories is being
released in a series of eighty books and audiobooks.
For an up-to-date listing of available titles,
go to www.goldenagestories.com.

AIR ADVENTURE

Arctic Wings	*Man-Killers of the Air*
The Battling Pilot	*On Blazing Wings*
Boomerang Bomber	*Red Death Over China*
The Crate Killer	*Sabotage in the Sky*
The Dive Bomber	*Sky Birds Dare!*
Forbidden Gold	*The Sky-Crasher*
Hurtling Wings	*Trouble on His Wings*
The Lieutenant Takes the Sky	*Wings Over Ethiopia*

FAR-FLUNG ADVENTURE

SEA ADVENTURE

TALES FROM THE ORIENT

MYSTERY

119

FANTASY

SCIENCE FICTION

WESTERN

The Baron of Coyote River   *Man for Breakfast*
Blood on His Spurs   *The No-Gun Gunhawk*
Boss of the Lazy B   *The No-Gun Man*
Branded Outlaw   *The Ranch That No One Would Buy*
Cattle King for a Day   *Reign of the Gila Monster*
Come and Get It   *Ride 'Em, Cowboy*
Death Waits at Sundown   *Ruin at Rio Piedras*
Devil's Manhunt   *Shadows from Boot Hill*
The Ghost Town Gun-Ghost   *Silent Pards*
Gun Boss of Tumbleweed   *Six-Gun Caballero*
Gunman!   *Stacked Bullets*
Gunman's Tally   *Stranger in Town*
The Gunner from Gehenna   *Tinhorn's Daughter*
Hoss Tamer   *The Toughest Ranger*
Johnny, the Town Tamer   *Under the Diehard Brand*
King of the Gunmen   *Vengeance Is Mine!*
The Magic Quirt   *When Gilhooly Was in Flower*

Charge into the Head of the Excitement!

American Eddie Moran is about to be captured in Morocco by the French Foreign Legion when bullets start flying at two strangers walking right towards him. Saving the men, Eddie learns that one is the American consul and the other is the recently deposed Berber leader, El Zidan. When a friendship forms between them, Eddie escapes the French with Zidan's help, only to be captured later and taken to the Atlas mountain stronghold of the Black Sultan, the cruel usurper of El Zidan's throne.

Not only must Eddie find a way out, he's bent on saving a beautiful American woman kidnapped to join a harem as one of the Sultan's many brides.

Get
The Black Sultan

JOIN THE PULP REVIVAL
America in the 1930s and 40s

Pulp fiction was in its heyday and 30 million readers were regularly riveted by the larger-than-life tales of master storyteller L. Ron Hubbard. For this was pulp fiction's golden age, when the writing was raw and every page packed a walloping punch.

That magic can now be yours. An evocative world of nefarious villains, exotic intrigues, courageous heroes and heroines—a world that today's cinema has barely tapped for tales of adventure and swashbucklers.

Enroll today in the Stories from the Golden Age Club and begin receiving your monthly feature edition selected from more than 150 stories in the collection.

You may choose to enjoy them as either a paperback or audiobook for the special membership price of $9.95 each month along with FREE shipping and handling.

CALL TOLL-FREE: 1-877-8GALAXY
(1-877-842-5299) OR GO ONLINE TO
www.goldenagestories.com
AND BECOME PART OF THE PULP REVIVAL!